The Puddle Dock Murders

The Puddle Dock Murders

Kevin McDonagh

Matador
Unit E2 Airfield Business Park,
Harrison Road, Market Harborough,
Leicestershire. LE16 7UL
Tel: 0116 2792299
Email: books@troubador.co.uk
Web: www.troubador.co.uk/matador
Twitter: @matadorbooks

ISBN 978 1803136 615

British Library Cataloguing in Publication Data.
A catalogue record for this book is available from the British Library.

Printed and bound in Great Britain by 4edge Limited
Typeset in 11pt Minion Pro by Troubador Publishing Ltd, Leicester, UK

Matador is an imprint of Troubador Publishing Ltd

For my parents, Annie & Joe

One

Brendan

A small crowd gathered by the Royal Exchange, adjacent to the Bank of England. A nearby clock had just chimed one. Over the noise of horse-drawn traffic, wagons and street sellers, a strong deep voice could be heard in the distance.

After a minute or two, an imposing figure strode forward and stood in front of the Exchange. A young lad placed a small wooden platform on the ground.

Brendan O'Carroll, the town crier for the City of London, effortlessly stepped onto the platform. The crowd shuffled nearer. He waited for the crowd to arrange and settle itself.

O'Carroll, resplendent in his gold and red uniform. His tricorn hat sitting squarely on his head. His gold buttons shone in the midday sun. His knee-length black boots were highly polished; only a veneer of dust on the uppers showed he had been walking for some time.

Not a stain or crease was allowed to besmirch the whole ensemble. He stood ramrod straight as he took out a parchment from his coat pocket. He unhurriedly took his spectacles from his top pocket and placed them on his nose.

He cleared his throat and then, with a theatrical flourish, stroked his moustache. The crowd roared its approval.

"Oyez, oyez, oyez. Murder, murder, murder. Strangler strikes in Puddle Dock." His baritone voice alerting all those near and far of the populace to the latest news.

The crowd had shuffled nearer to him. He towered over them and raised a hand for them to quieten down again.

He continued, "Sir William Thornton, murdered last night in Puddle Dock, Blackfriars. Strangled by person or persons unknown."

The crowd gasped at the news. It was likely that all but a few knew who he was, but the crowd had a part to play in the drama and were determined not to disappoint. Shouts of "Shame" and "Gawd help us" emanated from the throng.

O'Carroll continued, "Anyone having any information about this murder should speak to Sergeant Wales, at Snow Hill police station. A reward of ten pounds has been posted."

The crowd cheered as O'Carroll mentioned the reward. He then continued with the lesser news items. The crowd, having heard the important part of the news, began to disperse.

When he finished, he rolled the parchment up and placed it in his pocket. "God save the King," he exclaimed, as he moved off to his next allocated spot. The lad picked up the platform and followed him.

As the crowd begun to disappear, O'Carroll's voice was

heard repeating snippets of news as he walked to the next appointed stop.

After a long day walking the streets of the city, O'Carroll returned to his home in Whitechapel. His wife of twenty-five years, Mary-Jane, took his coat and hung it up. He sat at the kitchen table while she put a huge plate of Irish stew, his favourite, before him. The room was small and lit by a gaslight. It sputtered quietly.

In one corner was a kitchen with a gas stove. Opposite was a double bed. A curtain was drawn across from one corner to the next.

A door directly opposite the front door led to a landing which had steps down to a courtyard where washing could be dried and aired.

The kitchen table was situated in the middle of the room. Mary-Jane preferred to cook using the fire. The stove was expensive to run, and she avoided it whenever possible.

A magnificent mantelshelf emphasised the grate. A few cheap ornaments were placed on the shelf, memorabilia from trips to the seaside. A faded photo of the couple was placed in the middle of the shelf.

Next to the fireplace was a coal bucket, half full. Old newspapers were piled by the rear door. By the fire was an old leather armchair, it once was red in colour. Like the photo it was faded. This was Brendan's chair. Mary-Jane had a rocking chair which was set opposite.

A window completed the living space. It overlooked the street outside. It allowed light into the room and a breeze. The noise was constant. After a little while the couple did not notice the background noise.

The room was comfortable and homely. Even though the furniture had seen better days and the carpet fitted where it touched, it was scrupulously clean. Mary-Jane had done her best to make a home.

As she cut a wedge of bread for him, he sniffed the contents of the plate and smiled at her. Nothing was said. When he had finished, he wiped the plate clean with his bread.

Mary-Jane poured out a glass of ale into his pewter tankard, a present from his regiment when he retired. He rose from the seat and walked over to his chair by the roaring fire. Mary-Jane sat opposite him.

"Well, dearest, what news?" They both laughed. It was their joke. She fumbled in her pinafore for the letter which had arrived after lunch for him. Although she could not read, she recognised the town-hall crest.

He took it and looked at it for some time. It was important, that was obvious. Why would his employer send a letter? They could have waited until he had returned to the town hall.

Mary-Jane handed him a knife. He slit the top of the envelope and handed the knife back to her. He opened the slit and pulled the contents out. The paper was thick and of good quality. He took his spectacles out and read the contents. He sighed heavily.

He passed the letter to Mary-Jane. She folded it again and returned it to the envelope. She put in on the mantelshelf over the fire. She waited for him to tell her the contents.

"Well, my love, it looks like hard times may be coming. Brendan O'Carroll and wife, Mary-Jane O'Carroll, are likely destined for the poor house. My employers are determining my future at this moment. The learned aldermen of the council believe that they no longer need a town crier. It'll mean giving up this address and joining the masses on the streets. Twenty-five years of loyal service will be for nothing. I'm to meet the town hall clerk tomorrow."

Mary-Jane was quietly weeping. Brendan took her in his arms and comforted her. Later that night, Brendan undressed and slipped a nightshirt over his shoulders. He smoothed the wrinkles out and approached the bed. Mary-Jane was asleep. He quietly got into bed beside his wife. He looked across at her small figure. She slept with her mouth open; a problem with her sinuses that had never been treated.

Her health was deteriorating. The medicines she needed for her chest were expensive. Her sight was also a problem. She needed new glasses, but the cost was prohibitive in their present circumstances.

Without a full-time job, Brendan knew he would be unable to look after her medical needs. He turned away from her, frustration and anger welled up. He quietly sobbed.

Brendan O'Carroll was a large man. He was six foot five and strongly built. He had blue eyes and a huge moustache. His hair had been a shocking red, but, over the years, it had lost its vibrancy and had taken on a dull rusty hue.

Brendan could not sleep that night. He remembered when he had applied for the job as town crier. He was aware that the post often passed from father to son. He had arrived back in England from his service in India, only months before. It was the first job he had applied for. He did not count the army; his father had marched him down to the artillery recruitment office; he was twelve years old.

It had been a good life in the military. He left in eighteen-ninety-six after twenty-five years' service. He had met his future wife, Mary-Jane, a few months after landing at Southampton. She was the complete opposite of him. She could be described as petite. No more than five feet four in height, with an unremarkable face. Her hair was brown, with streaks of grey; cut into a fringe and shoulder length.

His one career regret was not being allowed to announce the death of the old queen, Victoria. It was a tradition that the steps of the Royal Exchange were used to announce certain royal proclamations.

Brendan was present when a royal herald announced the monarch's death and the succession of her son Albert, from the Royal Exchange steps, where he usually stood.

Brendan now sat on the bench outside the chief clerk's office in the town hall. He waited patiently. His tricorn hat was set neatly on his lap. He stared ahead. His boots shone brightly. No one could accuse Brendan of being untidy. His uniform was, as always, clean, and pressed. Mary-Jane was responsible for keeping his outfit in pristine condition.

The door opened and O'Carroll stood up. "Please come in, Sergeant Major," the clerk said. Brendan was pleased that he had used his former rank.

The clerk took his seat and said, "How long has it been? Twenty years?"

Brendan stood to attention and said, "Twenty-five years, sir. I've had the pleasure of being your town crier, sir."

Mr Hetherington smiled at Brendan and then quickly faded. This was the ninth person he had dismissed this morning. Some were summarily dismissed without an explanation, some like Brendan, deserved an explanation.

The clerk was tired. His health had been bad of late. His wife had left him weeks earlier. At fifty years old, he was a broken man. He had been losing weight lately and his appearance was of a depressed soul. His mind wandered. He suddenly remembered that Brendan was there.

"Of course, how time flies. All the council members appreciate your service. At the full council meeting last night, a motion was put forward and was passed unanimously, to award you a long-service medal. With thanks from the people of the City of London."

The sergeant major smartly stood to attention and said, "Thank you, sir. I'm honoured."

"The Lord Mayor has agreed to present the medal at the next full council meeting in person. A great honour indeed."

Brendan remained standing at attention. He guessed there was more.

"As you probably know, the newspaper industry has expanded quite considerably over the last few years. The literacy rate of the public has risen quite high. Many working people are now able to read." His tone suggested mild surprise.

"The honourable gentlemen of the council have concluded that the position of town crier is out of date for a modern institution, such as the City of London. They have decided to discontinue the position of town crier immediately."

Brendan showed no emotion at the news.

"Please hand in your uniform by Friday. I believe you also have a rent-controlled flat in Whitechapel. The council has decided to sell the property. You may stay there for a further two weeks. We at the City of London thank you for your outstanding service." He paused and said, "You are dismissed."

Brendan turned and left the office without another word. At home, he explained to Mary-Jane what had happened at the meeting.

She cleaned his uniform and hat for the last time and wrapped it in brown paper. She took it to the town hall the following day.

Brendan started to look for somewhere else to live. Luckily, he was a well-known figure in the city. Within the week, he had acquired a small flat in Blackfriars over the Queen's Head, a public house.

His next task would not be as quick. In his early sixties, he was still fit and strong, but jobs were difficult to get at the best of times. He and Mary-Jane had managed to save a small amount. If they used the money for the rent, it would last perhaps two months.

Mary-Jane could take in repairs; she was a trained seamstress. But she had her own problems. From five years old, she had been unable to speak. This had isolated her over the years. Many people who met her thought she was an idiot.

They married, both middle-aged, and were besotted with each other. Brendan also had a disability. Many years in the artillery had damaged his hearing, certain words were missed in conversations.

He could mask the hearing loss quite well. Besides, hearing problems were common in artillery regiments. He understood Mary-Jane's pain and frustration at not being able to converse normally. He sometimes realised that he was talking loudly. Not a problem in the army, embarrassing in civilian life; but perfect for a town crier.

The invitation to attend the council meeting where he would receive his long-service medal had arrived. He dressed in his army uniform. His row of medals were burnished and shone brightly. Mary-Jane had done her magic again.

The Lord Mayor of London pinned the medal onto his uniform and shook his hand. One press photographer took a photograph for the evening paper.

The medal looked inconsequential against O'Carroll's campaign medals. After the ceremony, he returned to his flat and Mary-Jane.

Brendan began to drink. At first it was just to pop downstairs for a quick glass of ale. After three months of idleness, it took him over. His resentment grew against the 'Nobs' that had taken away his job.

Mary-Jane worried but was unable to get through to him. He started to stay out late and come back in the early hours, smelling of drink and cheap perfume. All she could do was stand by his side and hope for a change for the better.

Six months had passed since his sacking. The police had arrested a vagrant for the murder of Sir William Thornton. It seems it was a street robbery that had gone bad. The culprit was hanged sometime later.

Brendan had found a job looking after a coal yard near London Bridge train station. He filled the coal bags for delivery by horse-drawn carts from a nearby company.

He walked home to Blackfriars Road. Some nights he walked across London Bridge. Other nights he walked through Borough Market to buy some fruit and veg for Mary-Jane.

When he was short of money, he would wait with the paupers and unemployed and collect vegetables which had been damaged or had been rejected by the customer.

Some of the vendors left a slightly better quality of veg; broken carrots, squashed cauliflower, or cabbages with dirty leaves; bruised fruit was always a favourite. Anything that the buyers did not want were left by the road.

Brendan was not ashamed to join the scrum to get the best vegetables from the rubbish piles.

It was on one such night that he was walking home after he had been able to acquire a box full of produce, he saw someone he thought he recognised. He followed the man toward the river by Puddle Dock.

The man sat on a bench and pulled his coat up and settled down. He lifted his legs and lay down on the bench.

Brendan stood over the prone figure. He did not speak, just watched him. The man felt his presence and immediately got up.

"Get away from me, I've no money for you."

Brendan said, "Is that Mr Hetherington, the town clerk? Fallen on hard times, have we?"

"Who's that?" he replied.

"Don't recognise me, hey? I'm your town crier. The one you dismissed."

"Oh, Mr O'Carroll, sorry, I didn't recognise you."

Brendan looked down at his clothes and boots. He was covered in coal dust. He knew his face was dirty.

"That's right, I'm a coalman now. No more smart uniforms. No more respect from my peers. Just another worker trying to make a living."

Mr Hetherington pulled his coat around him a little more. "It's cold tonight, don't you think?" He sat down again.

Brendan looked at him and said, "I suppose it is. What are you doing here? Why don't you go home to the warmth?"

Hetherington looked up at Brendan, "I have no home. I was evicted. Couldn't pay the rent. I was dismissed soon after you."

"I see, hungry?" He passed over an apple. Hetherington greedily took it, ignoring the rotten part, and bit into it. "Thank you. Nothing to eat all day."

"You know, I still remember your attitude as you dismissed me. You were so arrogant."

"Was I? I'm sorry. I was full of self-importance. How the mighty fall."

"Have you any prospects at all?" Brendan asked.

"At present, none whatsoever. I sleep by the river most nights. Come the winter, the cold will do me. I shall die, alone and unmissed. I was a very good clerk. Everyone said so…" He gazed out toward the river.

"You don't deserve it, but I going to help you." Brendan stood behind the bench. He put his fruit box down and placed his hands on Hetherington's shoulders.

Hetherington said, "Thank you."

O'Carroll's huge hands enclosed his neck. The fingers wrapped around his throat. The pressure increased.

Hetherington tried to struggle free, but then stopped and succumbed. His head lolled forward.

Brendan pushed him over and lifted his feet. He settled him onto the bench. He carefully wiped the coal dust away by spitting on his handkerchief and vigorously cleaning Hetherington's neck. He picked up his fruit box and walked home. He felt lighter and more content that he had for months.

Two

Conspiracy

Franz Mizel stood outside his small bookshop in Holborn. He was inspecting the damage to his windows. This was the third attack in as many months. Franz was a German émigré. This made him a target for many of his neighbours.

The reality was that he had been hounded out of Germany because of his opposition to Germany's militaristic aims. If this was known or even understood by the youths who had targeted him, it is doubtful that it would have made any difference. He was German and all Germans were suspect.

Franz had no money to repair the damage. He covered the windows with brown paper and flour glue. As an attempt to deter any further attacks, he glued a union flag to the bookshop's door.

The building was part of a parade of small businesses. It had accommodation above the shop. There was a yard out back. A dim light gave the shop the appearance of being open. Locals generally avoided it. Books were not a priority in Holborn.

Business was very slow. The only customers he had were either the curious, émigrés like himself, or police officers keeping him under surveillance.

Franz was well suited to the life of a book seller. He was now in his early sixties. Pot-bellied, his jacket could not be buttoned up in the front. He knew he was overweight, but it was not gluttony. His diet was based on what he could get from supporters or a book sale.

He was five feet nine inches tall. His hair was grey and very thin. His skin was dark with dark eyes. He had, in the past, used his stare to undermine an opponent. His teeth, those which were left after the many times he had been interrogated by Europe's secret police, were rotten.

A lifelong revolutionary, his bookish demeanour and soft-spoken manner hid a strong-willed and ruthless streak. Those who knew him were aware that it was a mistake to get on his wrong side.

His close friends were a diverse group of unemployed intellectuals. Once a week they would assemble at the bookshop for a meal and discussions about politics, revolution and any news gleaned from newcomers about European affairs. Mostly, anarchists used his shop to garner information. Tonight, Franz had his closest allies for the weekly evening meal.

Raul Santiago, a Spanish revolutionary. Saul Jacobs, Polish anarchist, married with one child. And Liam Cartney, a priest wanted by the British authorities, sat at a table laden with bread, margarine, apples and a small chicken. Raul had supplied everything except the bread and margarine; Franz had supplied those.

Raul was a very accomplished thief. He was never short of money. Many a meeting had been enlivened by a bottle of wine, biscuits, or a cut of meat. No one queried his largesse.

Franz welcomed his guests to his table, "Friends, fellow revolutionaries, welcome to my home. We meet as comrades in the battle for the freedom of the proletariat."

He lifted a glass of wine and toasted the revolution that was to come. They all smiled. Franz was known to be a bit pompous.

After the meal, they lit up their pipes and cigars. For a few minutes, each man was lost in his own thoughts. Saul was having trouble lighting his pipe. He banged the contents onto the table and then used a small penknife to scrape the inside of the bowl. He then packed it with the old tobacco.

A single gaslight spluttered and nearly went out. The light it gave off was hardly sufficient for the men to see each other. A dim glow enveloped their faces.

"Will they support us?" asked Liam.

Raul absentmindedly played with a piece of bread left after the meal. "I think so."

"With money and equipment?" Liam continued.

"They've pledged one thousand pounds. We can use the money to buy the necessary weapons and men," Saul answered.

The friends were quiet for a moment.

"Can they be trusted?" Franz interjected.

"They want England to be in a state of chaos. The conditions for revolution will be met. However, have no doubts, if we fail, they will come after us," Saul said.

Raul nodded. "They will kill us. They will want to make sure that no one will be left to implicate them."

Franz stood up and poked the fire. "Do we really need to ally ourselves with them? I have bad memories of the last time we met."

"We have a real chance to bring down this corrupt capitalist system and create the right conditions for the revolution. We all know what they did to you. But remember this, if England collapses, their allies will also face the wrath of the workers. Ireland and Europe will ignite in flames as the workers rise up and remove their oppressors."

Liam's eyes were blazing with fervour. They were silent for a while.

"Do we agree then?" Franz asked.

There was no dissent. Liam was given the task of collecting the money. Franz would act as paymaster. Raul and Saul were both experts in small arms, having been in their country's respective armies. They were tasked with training the recruits and organising the attack.

Liam and Franz sat by the fire talking. The others had left to go home.

"Could this be the beginning, what we've worked for all our lives?" Liam asked.

"It's a good plan. There's no reason to fail. If we keep the details confined to our inner circle," Franz replied.

They were silence for some time.

"Are we being naïve? The people who keep breaking my windows cannot be expected to understand the politics of revolution," Franz said.

"Don't be too hard on them. With the right education,

they'll understand why they have to live the way they do. With the right leadership, we can create a workers' utopia."

"I do hope so. I have spent my life being chased around the world, harassed by the secret police of many nations. But I have also seen acts of courage and charity from the poorest people. Some have died rather than betray me. This must work. I fear we will not survive. I am getting old. This may be my last chance. I will do whatever is necessary to bring this corruption to an end!"

Liam had no home or base. He slept where he could. Tonight, it would be in front of Franz's fire, tomorrow maybe a damp hedge. He never knew.

Franz threw a few pieces of coal on the fire. Liam said goodnight and snuggled under a blanket. The room was very warm. However, a draught from under the front door and ill-fitting windows made Liam's position uncomfortable. He inched nearer to the fire. Although still young, Liam never felt warm; too many nights under the stars had taken its toll.

Franz smiled at the prone body. He turned and went to his bedroom. He lay on the bed and pulled a blanket up to his neck. He leant over and turned the gas off. The flame flickered for a moment and went out. He listened to the traffic outside. He heard Liam snore gently.

The fire in the bedroom had gone out. He looked around and saw a mouse run across the room into a hole by the window.

"Nothing here for you, Mr Mouse."

Franz knew he would not sleep. Every sound jangled his nerves. Two voices outside were arguing. He moved to the bedroom window and looked out. The drunks were squaring up to each other. He returned to bed.

He closed his eyes. He tried to remember all the conspiracies he had been involved in over the years. Blurred faces raced into his mind. Friends and enemies had come and gone; murdered or locked up. He could not remember how many people he had killed. He knew that, at the time, it was justified. Now, he was not so sure.

He had been born in Germany but did not consider himself German. His family had moved around the continent. He spoke several languages; his first interaction with the authorities was in Dresden. He saw his father shot by a militiaman. He was twelve years old. His first arrest was aged sixteen. His revolutionary zeal was learned in a Russian prison.

He knew that he was getting old, his body would complain if pushed too far, he was aware that this was probably his last chance to change society. He was tired, physically and mentally. He closed his eyes. The front door was being tested. Was someone trying to get in?

Franz relaxed a little. He checked the clock; four am. He thought it strange the police were here. The doors were checked at least once a night. The constable was charged with randomly checking the doors of businesses. Nowhere in the world had he seen or heard of any other force doing that each night.

At last, Franz fell asleep. The last sound he heard was that of a police whistle being answered from afar.

Saul and Raul went their separate ways after leaving the bookshop. Saul went home to his wife and child. They lived in a tenement block next to the river in Bermondsey.

Despite his education, he was doomed to menial jobs, mostly day labour. He knew what poverty was. He did not need books to tell him what it meant. Revolution was not some utopian dream for him. It meant a better life for his children and everyone's children.

As he entered his flat, Saul saw the worried look on his wife's face.

"How's Agnes?" he asked.

Katya replied, "Burning up."

He could see she was exhausted. "Go to bed. I'll stay with her."

Saul held his daughter in his arms. She was breathing with difficulty. He touched her forehead; she was sweating profusely. Saul and Katya had lost two children from the fever. He hoped that this fever would break. They had no money for a doctor. If she survived the night, he would take her to the paupers' hospital near Tower Bridge. Saul started to hum a lullaby as he gently rocked his child. Katya smiled.

Saul and Katya had married young. For the first five years they had been chased across Europe by the forces of one or more secret services. After Katya got pregnant, they decided to go to England. They had hoped to leave the revolution to others, but it did not happen. They had a further four children, Agnes was the youngest. Their eldest was imprisoned in France. The second eldest had left home. They had no idea where he was. Two babies had died of cholera.

Saul was not a fit man. He had a persistent cough. Katya noticed blood in his handkerchief. Doctors at the free hospital had diagnosed tuberculosis. They both knew it was a death sentence. They did not have enough money to pay for medicines. He was told that he would be admitted if it got worse.

Raul walked toward Waterloo Bridge for about thirty minutes to ensure he was not being followed. He had a sixth sense about his safety, years being on the run in his home country had honed his senses. A quick glance in his direction or someone hurriedly walking away in the opposite direction always alerted him. Sometimes he would hop on a bus and get off at the last stop before finding his way home again. The weekly meetings were a necessary evil; useful, but at the same time, dangerous.

When he was satisfied all was clear, he hailed a cab and crossed the newly built Tower Bridge. He was dropped off at Newington Causeway. He walked toward Kennington, took another cab, and was dropped off on Brixton Hill. The surroundings were clean and well kept. The hill resembled a small village. Within its confines middle-class families were able to live a safe and protected existence. Raul entered a three-storey building with its neat front garden.

This was not the type of abode which a working man could afford. He entered the premises and was met by a maid, who took his coat and put it away. He washed and changed his clothes and went to bed. In the morning, he took a cab to Hyde Park. He sat on a bench and looked out across the park.

After some time, a smartly dressed man sat next to him. Nothing was said for a few minutes.

"What of our friends?"

Raul answered without looking at the man, "They are committed to the plan."

"Good, I will arrange for the money to be available for the pickup. Do you think they can do it?"

"Yes, they are determined. Cartney is the one pushing for action. The others are idealists. More at home in their books than taking direct action. However, with the right equipment, which I will get, they will have the best chance of creating the right conditions for us."

"They are, of course, expendable. Make sure that they do not live to tell the tale."

"Of course."

"Here is some money for your expenses." The man pushed a brown paper bag across the seat. Raul picked it up and walked away. The man waited a few minutes and walked away in the opposite direction.

Raul caught a cab and headed for the West End of London. The cab pulled up outside a large, three-storey building in Regent Street. A uniformed doorman opened the cab door and deferentially nodded at Raul; he was obviously known at the premises.

He alighted the steps to the establishment. The door opened quietly; Raul ignored the other uniformed man. He headed for the discreetly hidden casino. The money he had received from the man in Hyde Park soon disappeared. He had no luck that day.

He consoled himself with a visit to the third floor, where a gentleman could be entertained by a string of young beauties, available to service the client's every whim, for a price.

Raul stayed there for the rest of the afternoon. Refreshed and a little irritated at losing so much money, he determined to restore his finances with a little larceny and murder if necessary.

Three
Unidentified Body

Brendan arrived home later than usual. Mary-Jane saw the difference in him straight away. He smiled and as he gave her the box, she, in turn, took the fruit and put it in a bowl. The vegetables were put in the kitchen sink.

A large tin bath was sited in front of a roaring fire. Brendan stripped off his clothes and knelt in the bath. He was too large to sit. Mary-Jane took a copper kettle off the hearth and poured the heated water into a bucket. She followed the hot water with the cold. She tested it with her elbow. When it was at the right temperature, she poured it over his head and body.

He quickly lathered a block of soap and vigorously scrubbed his face, hair and then his body. Mary-Jane took the soap and washed his back, he stood up to allow access to his legs. He knelt and was rinsed off.

Mary-Jane held a blanket out and he dried himself off. Feeling refreshed, he dressed in his third-best clothes.

Brendan, despite working solidly for the last twenty-five years, still had very few clothes. His third-best clothes were used for everyday use, outside work. His second-best clothes were respectable but still a little threadbare. His uniform was saved for special occasions. Mary-Jane left him to empty the bath.

Due to their financial problems, Brendan had to make do with a bread and beef dripping sandwich and a mug of tea for breakfast. It was never enough for him; he always felt hungry. He would have been ashamed had he known that Mary-Jane was giving him the lion's share of the food.

The next morning, she took his work clothes to the communal drying area, strung a line between the two posts and began to beat them until the coal dust was removed. She left them to air.

After eating an apple, which left him still feeling hungry, he popped downstairs to borrow a newspaper from the landlord. Sitting with Mary-Jane, he read out the more salacious bits of news to her. He came across a 'stop-press' news item.

He read the piece quietly. Mary-Jane tugged his arm and smiled. He looked at her and said, "So sorry, dearest. 'Murder victim found in the Puddle Dock area. Police are investigating. More news midday edition.'"

Mary-Jane collected his clothes and retrieved her line. Brendan went out in his second-best suit to try and get more work. He returned downhearted after lunch. He had a nap until he was ready to go to the coal yard.

***

In Wood Street police station, Detective Inspector Ezra Theobald was tasked with finding the murderer of the corpse found on the bench in Puddle Dock. He was a veteran of the police service and relied on his instinct to catch the perpetrators of crime.

He was disdainful of the latest gadgets available to the new generation of detectives. He habitually dressed in black. He used a cane to help him walk, an injury from his army days.

At nearly six feet, he towered over his colleagues. His complexion was sallow with a thin face. His nose was the most striking feature. It was large, thin, and slightly hooked at the end. He was losing his eyesight. No one knew apart from the police doctor. He used a small magnifying glass when things were unclear. His teeth were black, a result of his regular pipe-smoking habit. He was sixty-four years old. Any talk of retirement was brutally rebuffed by him.

His one eccentricity was his hat. Unusually, he wore a workingman's flat cap. Still dark in colour. His contemporaries preferred a homburg or bowler. He walked over to the mortuary which was attached to the station but had its own entrance.

He stood over the body. "Good morning, Doctor. Do we know how he died?"

Dr Steadman carried on checking the body and did not look up.

"Definitely strangled. The body is that of a male, early fifties. He was eating an apple during the strangulation. Pieces were found in his mouth and throat."

"Manual or ligature?"

"Without a doubt, it's manual. Look at the bruising on his neck. It is very unusual."

The doctor pointed at the victim's neck; his hand was shaking.

"Why, Doctor?" The detective ignored the tremor.

"Well, he was strangled from behind. I haven't seen that before. I'll have more information after I have completed the autopsy."

Theobald smiled. "Good, that means it's unique. We just need to check if there're any other murders using that method. Thank you, Doctor."

Theobald turned away and walked to his subordinate.

"Meeks, find out if anyone has been murdered by strangulation, from the back."

"Sir?" Meeks seemed confused.

"The victim was strangled from the rear. Not the front, as would be expected. Understand?" He used his hands to demonstrate how.

"Oh, yes, sir." Sergeant Meeks ran off.

Later that afternoon, Dr Steadman was wiping his hands. DI Theobald entered the room. "What can you tell me, Doctor?"

The doctor stepped back as his assistant began to sew the chest of the corpse.

"The victim was a clerical worker; his hands and palms are soft. No callouses. He has not fed well recently. I would think that he had not eaten for at least a day, maybe two. His general appearance suggests that this period of want is recent. His clothes are of reasonable quality. He may have been robbed. I could find no watch or rings, yet there are signs. Watch chain in his pocket and marks on his fingers suggest a wedding ring."

Theobald was looking at clothes. "So, we have a married man, maybe divorced. Been gainfully employed until recently. He has not been eating or living anywhere. I'll have his photograph distributed. Someone should recognise him. Anything else, Doctor?"

"Yes, you're looking for a powerful man with big hands."

***

Brendan set off for work later that evening. He opened the coal yard and began to fill the bags. He lined them up when they were full. He checked the paperwork and ticked off the various orders.

He swept the yard around the filling machine. He filled one last bag. He lifted it and hid it behind a wall near the front gates. It would mean dismissal if he were caught removing it; maybe even prison if he was arrested.

He sat in the little office which was reserved for the filler. He ate a sandwich which Mary-Jane had made him. His hands were filthy with coal dust. His sandwich showed the marks of his fingers, nevertheless he continued to eat.

He opened a beer bottle and took a small swig of the contents. He hoped that it would last, at least until he had finished the rest of his work.

Every so often, he would look at the extra bag of coal. It was autumn. He could feel the cold seeping into his bones. Having spent twenty-five years in India, he was used to the heat. This season and the following months were purgatory to him.

He thought of Mary-Jane, he had noticed that she was coughing again. It always happened at this time of year. As if making his mind up, he said to himself, "She needs warmth and, by God, I'll ensure she gets it."

The Draymen were due to arrive at four o'clock. Brendan usually finished as soon as they were loaded. He pinned the paperwork to the board and looked around the yard. Everything was in its proper place.

After the coal was loaded, he checked the yard. He noticed a coalman's hat. It was brimless and had a long tail down the back. This was supposed to keep the coal dust from the neck. He tried it on. It was tight but he kept it anyway. Mary-Jane could alter it for him.

Brendan took a bag of coal home each week. He would use the hat as a disguise as he walked home. He hoped that those who saw him would think he was making a delivery. The coal that he did not need was sold to his neighbours. It made a few extra shillings for medicines for Mary-Jane.

***

DI Theobald and Sergeant Harold Meeks had now found the murder victim. He was Ernest Hetherington, a former town clerk. He had been dismissed for the loss of some old furniture which was thrown out. It should have gone to a second-hand shop, instead it was found in his back garden, covered with an old carpet.

It was inevitable that Theobald and Meeks would arrive

to interview Brendan. They were questioning all those workers who had been dismissed. Mary-Jane invited the police officers in. Theobald understood that she was dumb, but still tried to ask her questions.

At first, he thought she could not hear, so spoke loudly. She shook her head. He then passed over his notebook with a question. She shook her head again.

Theobald then said to Meeks, "It's no use, she's obviously an idiot."

Mary-Jane turned her back and walked away. Theobald looked at her retreating back and said, "Where's she going now? Follow her, Sergeant, quickly!"

Mary-Jane walked downstairs to the pub and found Brendan. She pulled his arm and looked at Meeks. Brendan walked toward him and said, "Something I can do for you?"

Meeks introduced himself and asked him to return to the flat. Meeks was feeling very small next to Brendan. Theobald had spent his time snooping around the flat.

Theobald and Brendan stood in front of each other. The detective was tall, but Brendan was taller; he was also bigger built.

Both detectives noticed O'Carroll's hands. Theobald knew he had his man.

"Do you know a Mr Ernest Hetherington?" Meeks asked.

Brendan answered immediately, "Town clerk. He arranged for my long-service medal before I left the town hall employ."

Theobald was staring hard at Brendan. He was hoping to pick up any nervousness from the suspect.

"I see," said Meeks, "so, there was no animosity between you and him?"

"None, whatsoever. Mr Hetherington was a gentleman of the old school; unlike so many today." Here, Brendan stared at Theobald.

Theobald asked, "Mr Hetherington dismissed you from your position as town crier, that must have irritated you?"

Mary-Jane was holding onto Brendan's arm as he replied, "The council members dismissed me. Mr Hetherington was just their mouthpiece. I understood why the council had to let me go. I have no problems with them or any of my former colleagues."

Theobald and Brendan were still staring at each other. Both unwilling to look away. Meeks interrupted. "Where were you on September twelve? In the early hours, say, four o'clock?"

"I was at work at the coal yard in White's Grounds by London Bridge station. I left just before four and walked home. It usually takes forty-five minutes."

"Anyone see you?" Theobald almost spat out the question.

Brendan smiled. "I should think so, I'm quite a big chap."

Meeks followed up with, "Anyone in particular?"

"Not that I know of."

"Very warm in here. Lots of coal, I see." Theobald was looking around the room.

"I work in a coal yard. I get it cheap. I'm allowed the dregs on the floor." Brendan now walked to the door and opened it. "Is there anything else I can do for you?"

"Not at present," Meeks answered.

They left the flat and Theobald called a cab. "Wood Street, cabbie." They both got in the carriage.

"Well, sir?" Meeks asked. "He fits the description Dr Steadman suggested, and did you notice his hands?"

Theobald lit his pipe. "I'm sure he is. But we need to get evidence. Put a tail on him. Have a word with the coal yard owners? Check his story out. If I can't get him for murder, by Jove, I'll have him for theft."

***

A week after the police interview, Brendan was called into the office to speak to the owner of the coal yard. Mr Simkins was a blunt man in speech and manner.

"I've had the police in here making enquiries about you. I'll have no truck with criminals in my employ. Explain yourself."

Brendan stood to attention. "Sir, I've done nothing wrong. I was asked about my whereabouts on September twelve. I was in the coal yard fulfilling my duties. I believe the officer was upset that I could prove my presence at work. He accused me of stealing coal. I told him that I had dregs only, sir. I pay the foreman for a bag of coal, occasionally."

Simkins called the office boy over. "Get Mr Houghton in here at once. And tell him to bring the sales receipts." The boy ran out and returned with the foreman, Mr Houghton.

"Houghton, have you received payment from O'Carroll for coal?"

He handed over the book with the pages that showed a payment on three occasions for a hundred-weight bag of coal. The cash had been entered correctly.

Simkins dismissed Mr Houghton. He looked at Brendan.

"I've no problem with my men purchasing coal. I do have concerns when police officers turn up at my offices. Ensure that this does not happen again. Or you will be dismissed. Understand?"

"Yes, sir," Brendan replied in his best parade ground voice. He turned and left the office.

At home, Brendan told Mary-Jane of what had occurred. She held his hand. He smiled. "So, dearest, what news?" She handed him the paper. They settled back as Brendan read the headlines.

One headline on page seven read, 'Detective Inspector Ezra Theobald confident of an arrest soon in the Hetherington murder case.' Brendan paused for a moment.

Mary-Jane leant across and took the newspaper from him. She smiled and folded it and put it by the fire for future use. They sat in silence holding hands, both deep in thought.

Four

Liam

Liam Cartney was nervous. He was carrying one thousand pounds in notes. He had never seen so much money in his life. He held on tight to the bag it was in. As he neared the bookshop, he thought he saw someone taking an interest in him. He walked past the shop and slipped into an alley and climbed the wall into the shop's backyard.

Franz closed the shop. He and Liam counted the money. It was sitting on the table in piles of fifty pounds. It was a fortune. Their backers were obviously serious in their intent. Each fifty pounds was wrapped in newspaper and put into a newly acquired safe, which had been fitted under the sink. A curtain hid it from view.

Franz pulled out a notebook from a drawer. "We need at least another eight others to help us."

"We need to pay them," Liam said.

"I know. I was thinking three shillings a week. It's better

than they would get working and it's not too much that it would draw the attention of jealous neighbours."

"Half a crown would be more than enough," Liam suggested.

"Fine, half a crown." Franz wrote in the book and continued, "What about us? Do we get a payment too?"

"In order to have the best chance to complete this task, we need to be fit. Last week the only proper meal I had was here, at the bookshop. The rest of the week I had to scavenge from the market leftovers. I feel the cold when I'm hungry. I get weak and can't concentrate."

"You are always welcome here," Franz said. Liam smiled.

"I thought I saw someone outside. It's dangerous for me to be seen in the same place too often."

"It is settled then. Five shillings a week for each of us. We will need money for travelling and research. Perhaps you can find somewhere to live?"

"Thank you. I know Saul will appreciate the money. Agnes is sick again. I spoke to him recently. He wanted me to say a prayer for her. Although I'm still a priest, I can't help thinking that I'm a hypocrite. Especially with what we're planning."

"Don't worry, we're all hypocrites. We talk about revolution without admitting through our actions many innocents will die. Did you pray with them?"

"Yes, he's my friend. How could I not?"

Franz wrote in the notebook again. "So, that is two pounds a week expenses. That is a lot of money. Do you think our backers will accept this?"

"If we account for every penny and get the job done. I see no problems."

"So, where do we get the eight men?" Franz asked.

"I know of several Irishmen who would be willing to join us. They know how to use weapons and they're no friends of the crown," Liam replied.

"Are they trustworthy?"

"I would trust them with my life."

"When you have them, Saul must agree. He is acting as security for the operation."

"No problem!"

They were quiet for a while.

"Do any of them know about boats? I mean your friends?"

"Boats? I thought you had dismissed the water idea."

"I cannot see how we can get near enough to attack him otherwise. A motor launch of some type would get us within striking distance."

Liam was shaking his head. "It would also make us a sitting target. Any hope of getting away would be gone. They would blow us out of the water."

Franz smiled. "I have no illusions. I do not expect to come out of this operation alive."

"I agree."

Liam opened a beer bottle and poured the contents into two cups. He passed one to Franz. "You know, I've expected to be caught, many times. I suspect I'll end up either in a gutter, shot by the crown forces or hanged in the Tower. Despite this I still hope and believe that I can lead my fellow Irishmen to freedom one day."

"You are still young. Optimism is your shield. I've lost many friends. My wife and children died because of me. I'm tired of running. Tired of trying to persuade people that my vision will make their lives better. If I cannot persuade them, then I must make them."

***

Detective Inspector Maurice Holcombe was reading several reports which arrived on his desk each morning. He was newly promoted Inspector in the Special Irish Branch of the Metropolitan Police. His task was to keep tabs on Irish rebels in London. However, over the last few years, the SIB had also begun to expand into other areas.

London was a magnet for people hiding from repressive governments on the continent. Anarchist numbers had grown, and with it, political protest and dissension.

In his mid-forties, Maurice Holcombe had worked hard for his promotion. He was a Freemason and an Elder in the Church of Scotland. He also proudly wore his father's sash. Despite being born in Blackburn, England, he was the archetypal Scot. His hair was a sandy colour. He had piercing deep-blue eyes. He was pale skinned and had a huge moustache that joined his sideburns.

He noticed a report on an Irish rebel by the name of Liam Cartney. It was reported that he had been seen around the Holborn area. He was wanted in Ireland and had many friends and associates in the Fenian ranks.

He called the records division for the full file on Cartney. By the time he had read it, he had decided that Liam Cartney would be his first arrest as an inspector in the SIB. Technically, Liam Cartney was still a priest. This irritated

Holcombe. All his prejudices welled up. Men of the cloth should not be involved in sedition.

***

Raul introduced a young German anarchist to Franz at the bookshop. "This is Udo. He's a mariner. He knows boats and can help us get the right one for the job."

Franz smiled. "You're very young. Where did you get your experience of boats?"

"My father is a fisherman. I went out with him all the time. I joined the navy, but we disagreed about my role. I had to depart, quickly."

"You're on the run, yes?"

"I jumped ship when we visited Glasgow. I've been running for a year."

Franz patted him on the arm. "Please wait in the shop for a minute."

Udo walked away and looked at the books. Franz watched him.

"Can you trust him? He appears to be very well fed for someone who has been on the run for such a long time."

Raul replied. "I know his uncle. We were imprisoned in Germany in ninety-six. He's fit because he comes from money. His father owns a fishing fleet in Bremen. He's being subsidised by his family. His father used to help the cause by ferrying comrades in and out of Germany."

"Still, keep an eye on him. Under no circumstances should he be told of the whole plan."

"Of course."

"Udo, please join us. We need a boat. It should be able to carry at least twelve. Can you find something for us?"

"I'll ask my contacts in the ports. It could be expensive."

Raul said, "Leave the money to us. Let me know when you have picked one. We'll look at it."

"Do you need any money?" Franz asked.

"No, It's fine. My family looks after me." Udo left by the back door.

"He speaks English well. Just a slight accent on certain words. With his fair hair, blue eyes, and physique, he could pass for an Englishman. Good food and fresh air will always count. In fact, with the right uniform, he could also pass for a Junker," Franz mused.

"Let's see if he is as good as we think. I can follow him if you're in any way worried about him?" Raul offered.

"Perhaps, until we are surer."

"If he's an informer, I will cut his throat and drop him in the Thames," Raul said.

"Only as a last resort. I do not like violence for violence's sake," Franz replied.

"It is necessary. I spent many years in jail because I was squeamish. I will never make that same mistake."

Raul collected his hat and bade Franz goodbye.

Udo was waiting for Raul by Ludgate Circus. They walked off together, across Blackfriars Bridge.

***

Liam Cartney had managed to rent a small room in Covent Garden. It overlooked the market. It was bustling with people at all times of the day and night. He could mix with the locals and come and go as he pleased.

He walked to Petticoat Lane and used part of his first five shillings to buy himself some second-hand clothes. As he bundled up his purchases, he saw two men looking at him. He guessed that they were police officers. He quickly walked into a crowd and pushed his way through.

When he got into the most crowded part of the market, he shouted out, as loud as possible, "Watch out, the cozzers are here."

The crowd immediately started to panic and ran off in all directions. The sellers picked up their wares and tried to flee. Petticoat Lane was still classed as an unofficial market. The sellers were aware of the fines that could be imposed.

Liam ran with a group of people carrying their stock. The two officers were identified almost immediately. They could not follow him in the mayhem.

He managed to get away this time. He realised that someone was targeting him. He decided to forego his weekly meetings until he could be sure of his safety. He stayed indoors for a couple of weeks before he ventured out.

Liam saw a youngster playing by some swings. He approached him. "Do you want to earn some money?"

The lad eyed him suspiciously. He was dressed in short trousers, a coat two sizes too big and shoes open at the front, probably due to kicking a ball, or more likely, stones.

"You sure, mister? I can get me sister if you like. Cost ya a tanner." He wiped his nose with the sleeve of his coat. He coughed uncontrollably for a few seconds.

"No, I need this message taken to Holborn. Can you do it?"

"That's a long way, mister, how much?"

"I'll give you a farthing." He held the coin up.

"Nope, cost ya a ha'penny, at least."

"All right. Here, can you read?"

"A little."

"It's the bookshop opposite the tobacconist. Give it to the small man only. I'll know if you don't do it. I'll come and find you and beat you, understand?"

The lad took the money and the note and ran off in the right direction. Twenty minutes later and out of breath, he arrived at the bookshop. As he went forward, he was pulled aside by a tall man.

"What you up to?" The plain-clothed officer asked.

"Got to deliver a note. The man said I'd be given a ha'penny, for my trouble."

"Let's see it," the officer demanded. He held on tight to the lad's arm.

The lad said, "What about my money?"

"You'll get a clip round the ear. Hand it over."

The officer read it and copied the message into his notebook.

"All right, go and deliver it and no telling anyone that I saw it."

The lad entered the bookshop. Franz looked at him and said, "Hello, may I help you?"

"Got a note for you." He handed it over. "Man said you'd give me a ha'penny for my trouble."

"Did he?"

Franz read the note and then tore it up and put it in the fireplace. He opened the till and reached for a farthing. The lad saw it and said, "If you make it a ha'penny, I tell you what the copper outside wanted."

"Yes, that seems fair. What did he want?"

The lad left the shop and ran toward home. In his pocket were two ha'pennies.

Franz began to collect his possessions. He put the money in a box which he hid at the bottom of a crate. He wrote out a note and pinned it to the inside window. It read, 'closed for a week, bereavement.'

He waited until it was dark. He loaded the crate onto a trap which had arrived at the back of the yard. During the night, Franz quietly left the bookshop. The watchers were unaware that he was gone.

Five

The Nark

DI Theobald had decided to have Brendan followed. He passed the task to Meeks who used one of his narks, a petty thief called Erskine. He was soon following Brendan each evening as he went to work. He noted how long he stayed at the coal yard, who he spoke to and, on occasion, when he knew his target was away, buy drinks for the regulars at Brendan's pub, while pumping them for information.

Brendan was told of the little man who had been asking questions. He noticed that he was being followed. He decided to do something about him.

The following day, he bought a bag of coal. Mr Houghton left the receipt on the board to pick up later that night when Brendan came in. After completing his tasks, he filled his bag and put it by the gate, as usual.

Erskine noted the coal bag and decided on a plan to get his own. A little bit of blackmail was normal fare for him. He followed Brendan as he carried the bag on his back. They walked at a steady pace down to the river near Blackfriars Bridge.

Brendan continued to the embankment near Puddle Dock. It was a cold night, no one was around. He sat on a bench near to where Mr Hetherington had met his fate. He waited until the small man was very near. Erskine sat next to him.

"Cold tonight, mister. Yes, very cold. Is that coal, mister? Where'd you get it? I suspect the police would also like to know?"

Brendan turned to look at him and smiled.

Erskine continued, "I could take half a bag from you, mister. No one need know. Then perhaps you could get me a full bag each week; until it gets warm. What d'you say?"

Brendan replied, "Why would I give you my coal?"

"Well, I know a cozzer by the name of Meeks. He works at Wood Street. He's a detective sergeant. He wants info on you. I can tell him good things or bad. It depends on my mood. When I'm warm, I'm always in a good mood. Not so much when I'm cold."

Brendan moved a little closer to Erskine, who immediately pulled a knife out. "That's as near as you need to be, mister. Have we a deal?"

"Okay, the bag's heavy. I could do with making it lighter. Will you help me? I have a spare on top of the bag."

Erskine peered into the coal bag and saw the spare. "Okay, no tricks. Fill it halfway. I'm not greedy." Erskine held his bag open while Brendan upended his. The coal poured in. When they had agreed on the share, Brendan said, "Meet me tomorrow and I'll have another bag for you."

Erskine said, "A full one."

"Of course. Better bring a trolley. They're heavy." They agreed to meet at four o'clock.

Mary-Jane sat by the kitchen table sewing a huge sack out of old flannel. She held it up and then turned it inside out. Brendan looked at Mary-Jane and smiled. "That'll do fine, dearest."

The sack was wrapped up in brown paper. Brendan tied it to his lunch pail. At work, he made sure the contents were not exposed to the coal dust.

At two o'clock, he filled a bag of coal to the top. This would be for Erskine. In the second one, he half-filled it and padded it out with empty bags.

The coal bags were put in the usual place. At four o'clock, Erskine appeared by the gates. He had waited until the last dray had left. He looked over toward the bags and chuckled to himself.

"I see you're a man of your word, mister."

"Where's your trolley?" Brendan enquired.

"It's here on the pavement."

The gate was opened, and Erskine pulled the trolley over to the sacks. He tried to lift the bag onto his trolley but gave up.

"Give me a hand," he demanded.

Brendan pushed him out of the way and lifted the bag onto the trolley.

"Here's a receipt just in case we get stopped. Follow me and it'll look like I'm helping you with a delivery," he said.

The gate was locked, and they both walked toward London Bridge. Erskine pulled the trolley along, while Brendan carried the half-filled bag on his back.

"Where we going?" asked Erskine, after following Brendan for half an hour.

"Down by Puddle Dock. I've got the use of a shed. We can put the coal there and you can pick up as much as you want when you want it. I've got you an extra key."

Erskine, ever wary of people doing him favours, shouted, "No tricks, or else, mister."

They stopped in front of a small door in a rundown building. It was deserted and due for demolition. Erskine relaxed when he was given the extra key. He stepped forward and lit an oil lantern.

As he placed the lantern on a shelf just inside the door, Brendan stepped up behind him and grabbed him around his neck. Erskine was lifted off the floor.

His grip on the smaller man was tightened. Despite Erskine kicking out and trying to stab at his attacker, he slowly passed out. The knife fell to the floor.

Throughout the incident, Brendan gave no sign of emotion. He concentrated on squeezing the breath out of Erskine. When he felt the body go limp, he dropped it to the floor.

Very quickly, he retrieved the coal receipt from the body. He then took out Mary-Jane's sack. He manhandled Erskine into it. He tied the neck with a piece of string. Looking around, he could see no one.

Brendan had thought to leave the body with the coal in the little room and dispose of it later. A Thames mist started to envelop him. He placed the body on the trolley and pulled it towards the embankment. There was a set of steps which led down to the river.

He lifted the body out of the trolley and carried it to the top of the steps. He untied the bag and removed it. He threw the body forward. It hit the bottom step with a thud. He heard a gasp of air escape from the body. He descended the steps. He gave it a push with his boot. It rolled down until it hit the foreshore.

He lifted the trolley and threw it after Erskine's body. Both were already wet from the river's tide by the time he had walked away.

He hid the half bag of coal inside the building with Mary-Jane's sack. He carried the full bag home.

The Thames tide lifted the body and carried it away. By the time it was noticed, under Blackfriars Bridge, it was battered and disfigured.

It was found in the detritus on the foreshore. A worker noticed it as he walked to work early one morning.

The police doctor was examining the body. He was attempting to focus his eyes, but the effects of the previous night's drinking bout were making it difficult. His hands were shaking.

His assistant was looking at the body and describing the injuries. DI Theobald arrived and noted the doctor's condition. He knew that Dr Steadman was prone to hit the bottle from time to time. He spoke to him.

"What can you tell me?"

The doctor tried to speak but his answer was slurred. Theobald looked at the assistant and raised his eyebrows.

"It's a drowning. The body has been drowned. The damage is from hitting the concrete and the gravel on the shoreline," the assistant replied.

Theobald looked at the doctor, who managed to say, "I agree, drowning." He then threw up.

Theobald walked away and spoke to Meeks. "The doctor's unwell, go back to the mortuary with the body. Try and find out if it was a drowning. When the doctor is well, perhaps we'll get a clearer account of what happened."

Theobald and the doctor had been colleagues for over fifteen years. His problems with the bottle arose after his wife died.

Theobald had covered for him on many occasions. Shoddy post-mortems and evidence missed were quietly overlooked. However, since the force had begun to modernise, covering his incompetence had become harder.

Meeks waited in the mortuary. The doctor was busy elsewhere; Meeks knew he was lying down in his office. The assistant was undressing the body and making a note of the contents of the pockets. Meeks walked over and watched the man meticulously note everything down. His handwriting was neat and legible, unlike the doctor's.

The assistant was emptying the coat pocket of the victim. He removed a small knife, some five inches long, single blade. Bone handle.

Meeks stepped forward, "May I see that?"

The assistant gave him a pair of gloves to wear. He saw Meeks' confusion.

"Could be evidence."

Meeks pulled a face. But he put them on and picked the knife up. He peered at it closely. He opened the blade and saw what he was looking for.

"Did you find another knife? Perhaps bigger, bone

handle, maybe seven inches. A sheath knife?"

"Not at the moment," the assistant answered.

Meeks removed a small sheet that was covering the face. He scrutinised it for some time. It was badly disfigured. Its face was a mass of bruises and bloated from the water. Meeks shook his head.

He scrutinised the neck.

"Could he have been strangled?"

The assistant took a magnifying glass and looked at the neck.

"It's possible. We'll know after the doctor returns…from his paperwork."

Both men were quite comfortable with the lie.

Meeks returned to the scene of the incident.

Puddle Dock was only about a half a mile away. Could this new incident be associated with the murder of Hetherington? If he were correct about who the body was, it could be the proof they needed.

The body could have been washed further along the river. The damage to the body could be, as the assistant had said, caused by the concrete fixtures along the river.

He looked down at the foreshore and suddenly smiled. If it was Erskine, the chances were good that O'Carroll had murdered him. Probably to stop him picking up any evidence in the original murder.

Meeks rushed back to the mortuary. Theobald was not pleased that he had disappeared without informing him. His demeanour changed when Meeks explained his theory.

They stood around the body on the slab. The doctor and his assistant were dressed to start the autopsy. Theobald looked at the doctor. He noticed that he was allowing the assistant to start the first incision.

"Feeling better, Doctor?" he said. Dr Steadman ignored the implied criticism.

The doctor quietly instructed his assistant to make a cut here and then there. The lungs were removed. They were full of water. The doctor instructed the assistant in what to look for. Meeks could no longer contain his patience.

"Doctor, was the victim strangled?"

Steadman stopped and looked at Meeks. "I will give my report after I have completed my autopsy. Please, Sergeant Meeks, contain yourself."

Suitably chastened, he walked away from the table and muttered to himself. Theobald knew how the doctor hated being interrupted, so remained quiet, watching the medics work away at the body.

After an hour, Dr Steadman approached DI Theobald. "The deceased died of drowning. His lungs were full of water."

Theobald nodded. "What of the bruises on his neck?"

"In my opinion, he was strangled. But I'm sure he was not dead before he was immersed in the river."

Meeks had joined his boss. "Are there any similarities between Mr Hetherington's and this body?"

"If you're asking if the same person strangled Hetherington, I would have to say yes. The bruising on both bodies is almost identical."

Theobald smiled and said, "Thank you, Doctor. Meeks, arrest Brendan O'Carroll for murder."

Six

The Baron

Udo knew his business. He, Raul, and Franz were inspecting a steam-powered launch. It was at least twenty years old. It had been well used in the past. The seller started the engine. It was quite noisy. Smoke and steam billowed from the engine, which seemed to stutter as it slowly reached full steam.

They moved away from the engine and looked at the cloud of smoke pumping into the air.

"We'll be seen for miles. How can we get close to the target with that racket going on?" Raul said.

"Udo, can you make it run quieter and with less smoke?" Franz asked.

"It would need to be stripped down. Then perhaps new parts. It may not be worth the time and trouble. What do you need it for?"

Raul interjected, "Nothing you need to know, yet."

"That's of no use," Franz said. "We need something

49

quieter and bigger. I'm told that steam is fast being replaced by diesel engines."

"The cost would be far too much," Raul said.

"What about our sponsors, could they get one for us?" Franz persisted.

"I can ask. They may be willing."

Udo returned from looking over the vessel. "The wood's rotten, he was trying to trick us. I'm not sure it could take the weight of twelve men. No, it's no good." He wiped his hands as he walked away. The others followed him.

Franz pulled Raul aside. "A launch is definitely too small. We have twelve men, plus all the munitions and we need somewhere to fire from. We would be too exposed. No, we will have to change the plan."

"Do you have a better idea?" Raul asked.

"Perhaps a fishing boat? Or one of the pleasure crafts that use the river. It must be able to mix with the other craft that are likely to throng around the target."

"Please investigate the possibility of a bigger boat," Franz said to Raul.

***

The following Sunday, Raul was seated at the same bench in Hyde Park. The well-dressed man from their previous meeting sat next to him. Near enough to be heard, but not too near that a passer-by would think they knew each other.

"Well?" he asked. "What news?"

"We have hit a snag, Herr Baron."

"Explain."

"The boat idea has resurfaced. Franz insists on getting a bigger boat. I tried to dissuade him, but he believes that we need a more substantial platform to succeed. Something that can handle a bigger crew and arms."

"What does our mariner friend say?"

"Udo thinks a bigger vessel would be more stable, more able to withstand any retaliatory gunfire."

"So, what is the problem? They have enough money, do they not?"

"I worry that the more people know about it, the less security we have."

The baron was silent for a minute.

"So far there are four players in the conspiracy. And, of course, me. Our friends in the Friends of Hibernia know nothing yet. At some time, I should let them know. After all, we will be using their men for the attack. I see no reason to worry, yet. Stay vigilant. Remove anyone you think is a security risk."

Raul left first. The baron got up a few minutes later. He walked slowly to the park entrance, where a carriage was waiting for him.

"The office!"

Baron von Marburg was the head of the Kaiser's secret service in England. A Prussian aristocrat of the old school. He allowed no dissent from his subordinates.

His personality was cold. His hair was shaved closely. He had a duelling scar across his cheek. He was proud of it. Although in his early fifties, he was still fit and strong. With striking blue eyes and a thin moustache over a slightly turned-down top lip; he appeared to be scowling all the time. He had the air of someone in authority. Exceedingly ambitious, he was determined that the plan would work, no matter the cost.

Aloof at all times, he kept his own counsel. The upcoming attack was his idea. He knew if it failed, the Kaiser would have him publicly executed.

The baron was a veteran of the 1870–71 Franco-Prussian war. France was humiliated and a united Germany became the effective power in Europe. As a young man he revelled in the war, its glamour, honour, patriotic fervour, and plaudits bestowed by the emperor Wilhelm.

The baron knew that Germany's territorial ambitions would fail unless England and its empire was destroyed. It had taken several years to set the plan in motion. It is difficult to know how much the Kaiser knew.

The baron was using his own wealth to pay for the attack. If it succeeded, he could expect to be a very important man in Germany, and perhaps governor of the newly acquired territory of England.

Seven

The Interrogation

DI Theobald was not going to allow the lack of evidence to get in the way of a conviction. He was sure that O'Carroll was guilty. He would sweat the truth out of him.

Meeks and two constables arrived at O'Carroll's flat above the Queen's Head pub in Blackfriars Road. The horse-drawn Black Maria soon became the centre of attraction for passers-by.

Brendan was escorted out in handcuffs. He was put in the Maria and driven away. Mary-Jane was in tears and being comforted by the landlady.

Wood Street was the headquarters of the City of London Police. Theobald was well known to the other officers. Most detested him. His arrogance was well known. However, he did get convictions, so his superiors tolerated him.

Within Wood Street, many of the officers were ex-army. A high percentage were also of Irish descent. Brendan

O'Carroll was well known to them from his town-crier duties. A few had been in his regiment. Everyone knew that he was a decent man; all were sure he was not a murderer. They were also sure he was being set up by Theobald.

Brendan sat in an interrogation room. It was lit by gaslight. It was dim, cold, and dingy. Wood Street was waiting to be upgraded to electric lighting. Theobald preferred to use this last bastion of gloom to break his suspects. He thought the enclosed atmosphere was better to wear them down.

Theobald and Meeks entered the room. Meeks stood while Theobald got to the point. "I know you killed two men. Strangled them. Disposed of the bodies. Took Hetherington's watch and rings. What do you say to that?"

Brendan stared at Theobald and said, "The only men I have killed were killed on Her Majesty's orders; in the service of my country."

"I have a doctor who will swear that your hands are the same size as the murderer's and will fit the bruises. What do you say to that?"

"I say again, I've not killed anyone."

Meeks then stepped forward. "My man told me that you were stealing coal from your employer. He said you were going to deal him in."

"So, I'm a murderer and a thief? Bring in your witness, let's see him." Brendan smiled.

"He's dead. Murdered by you."

"Very convenient, I would say."

Theobald stepped forward and put his face up to Brendan's. "You're not leaving here until I get a confession, do you hear me?"

There was a knock on the door, Theobald shouted, "What!" A well-dressed gentleman entered the room.

"Detective Inspector Theobald? Good afternoon, my name is Jonathan Treadway. I am Mr O'Carroll's solicitor."

"How the hell can a coalman have a solicitor? It doesn't make sense," Theobald shouted.

"Well, this one has. I am retained by the Friends of Hibernia, a charity for ex-servicemen of Irish descent. Now, I would like to speak to my client, alone."

Theobald and Meeks left the interrogation room. They were fuming. "How did they find out about this case?" Meeks asked. They looked around and saw several constables smirking.

"Of course, I should have guessed. Always stick together the boyos do," Theobald spat out. As they walked away, they heard laughing.

After half an hour, Mr Treadway asked to see DI Theobald.

"My client states that he is not guilty of the crimes you have accused him of. Therefore, I have advised him not to say anything. If you try to speak to him without my presence I will certainly speak to your superiors."

Theobald was a broken man. His plan relied on bullying the suspect. He had no real evidence.

"Please inform Mr O'Carroll that he is free to go," Theobald said sullenly.

He had decided to take a different route to get what he wanted. He watched as the solicitor and O'Carroll walked out of the station. Several constables were waiting to shake their hands.

Meeks or Theobald had contacted Brendan's boss about the arrest. When he arrived for work, a guard met him and took his keys away. He was dismissed.

He had been able to amass a reasonable amount of coal. He had it hidden in the derelict building near Puddle Dock. Brendan thought it likely that the police would be following him.

After two weeks, his coal was running out. He had no other choice than to go to Puddle Dock and retrieve a bag of coal. He left his flat at midnight.

As he made his way to the coal, he kept looking behind him to ensure no one was following. He arrived at the derelict building and slipped behind a newly erected fence.

As he lifted the bag out, Meeks stepped in front of him. "You're under arrest for theft." He held out his handcuffs and tried to put one on Brendan. It was futile.

Brendan pushed his hand away and clamped Meeks in a bear hug. He could not move and tried to wriggle from the grip. It was difficult to breath. Brendan increased the pressure. Meeks could feel himself slowly losing consciousness.

He allowed Meeks to slide to the floor. The prone figure lay crumpled in a heap. He was still breathing, albeit very shallow. Brendan was now in a quandary. This was a policeman. It was likely that his superiors knew what he was doing.

He had a difficult choice. If he let him go, he would find himself incarcerated in prison. Perhaps the police could prove he had murdered Erskine and Hetherington, in any case, they would have him for attempted murder of a police officer. He needed time to think.

Meeks was tied up, gagged, and placed behind the coal

bags in the building. Brendan lifted a coal bag and placed it by the fence. He locked the door, lifted the bag on his shoulders and walked home.

Meeks woke up as the sunlight seeped through the door. He tried to move but was firmly held by the ropes. The coal bags were set around him like a cell. He knew they were too heavy to move. He tried kicking them. He then lifted his feet and tried steady pressure to move them. He gave up. He was caught.

Over the years that Brendan and Mary-Jane had been married, they could communicate with each other as well as any married couple. Mary-Jane knew there was something wrong.

She sat next to him and gently put her hand on his cheek. He looked at her. "I'm sorry, dearest. I can't." He looked away. She tugged on his arm. He knew she would not stop until he explained.

"It's the gallows for me. I'm a murderer." She squeezed his hand. He continued, "I killed two men. I killed Mr Hetherington, the town clerk who dismissed me. I don't know why. But I know I enjoyed strangling him. I felt relieved. As if a great weight was lifted. The other one was a copper's nark, he tried to blackmail me."

She leant across and kissed him.

"I'm so sorry, dearest," he said. "I don't know what to do."

She looked into his eyes; he knew that he had to tell her everything. He told her of Erskine and of Meeks. She nodded that she understood.

***

DI Theobald was getting increasingly irritated by Meeks' disappearance. He had no idea where he was or what he was doing. After a day, Meeks was still absent. Theobald issued an APB. Every officer in London was told to find him.

Mary-Jane had been thinking over how to help her husband. She had a plan. She woke Brendan. They both dressed. She pushed him out of the door. It was after midnight. They walked to Puddle Dock.

Brendan showed her the door where Meeks was being held. Mary-Jane motioned to the door. Brendan opened it. She lit the oil lamp and held it over the bags. She peered in and saw Meeks. He was wriggling and trying to speak. She blew the lamp out and stepped back and Brendan locked the door again. They walked home together.

Brendan wrote a note. 'I know where Meeks is meet me three o'clock tonight at Puddle Dock come alone.' His handwriting was neat but childlike.

Mary-Jane waited by Wood Street. She saw DI Theobald come out of the police station. He called for a cab. Just as he was telling the cabbie where to go, she threw the note through the carriage window and walked quickly away.

Theobald sat back in the cab and rested both hands on his cane. He noticed the note on the floor. Picking it up, he read it and at once told the cabbie to stop. He looked out of the window. The street was busy with people coming and going. He had no idea who had left the message.

DI Theobald was no fool. He knew better than to turn up at a clandestine meeting without backup. He returned to the police station and retrieved his revolver. He loaded it and fitted it in his pocket.

Meeks was getting weaker by the minute, he had been without food or water for thirty-six hours. He had a headache, and his tongue was swelling in his mouth. His extremities were pale and bloodless. He heard a noise outside the door. His hopes rose.

Mary-Jane opened the door and lit the lantern again. She stared at Meeks. Although his blindfold kept him from seeing, the light still crept under and hurt his eyes. The breeze allowed the cold air to waft over him. He began to shiver.

Mary-Jane waited by the fence. In the distance, she heard the clip-clop of a horse coming nearer. The noise stopped for a moment and then started up again.

Theobald saw Mary-Jane by the fence. He walked up to her and handed over the note. She nodded and walked in front. He followed her. His free hand was on his pistol in his pocket. The ground was uneven. He was leaning on his cane for support.

She pointed to the doorway. Theobald pulled the gun out and motioned her to move away. He had to momentarily put the gun away as he went in through the door. He saw Meeks and leant forward to pull the blindfold off.

At that moment, Brendan closed the door on them. He ran around to the side and started to hit the supporting wall with a sledgehammer. After several hits, the building began to shake.

A pistol shot reverberated as Theobald tried to shoot at the lock. It was followed up by several more. Brendan continued to hit the wall. There was a loud crack as it gave way. Brendan ran away as fast as he could.

The building collapsed and tons of masonry fell on top of the little room where Meeks and Theobald were.

Brendan and Mary-Jane walked away hand in hand. They turned as the whole row of buildings collapsed. Where, five minutes ago, they had been standing, the whole area had been covered by rubble.

It was another six months before the bodies were found.

Eight

Co-Conspirator

Mary-Jane was a traditional housewife. While Brendan went out every day, she shopped, cooked, and cleaned their home. For Brendan it was days of meeting people, enjoying the sunshine, and knowing that he had respect from those he met.

Every day was a battle for Mary-Jane. Her inability to communicate was a major frustration for her. Those who met her were convinced she was an idiot. They tried to cheat her and fob her off with inedible cuts of meat, short-change and disrespect her.

Despite her passive nature she was capable of fits of temper worthy of any man. Her problems with reading were as a result of losing the ability to speak, not her general intelligence. When it came to counting, she was above average. Numbers held no fear for Mary-Jane. Counting did not need the same skills as reading.

Mary-Jane had witnessed a family member being gored

by a bull on their farm. From that day she had not been able to speak. The local doctor had no idea what to do. Her parents were unable to help her. Sometimes she would daydream and be lost to the world around her. Her teaching effectively came to a halt.

She would listen to her father discussing the day's business. All of the gossip, which she would not be privy, used to make her laugh. Now, she could not join in. Her father and mother would speak to each other as if she was not there. His words were never cruel. They spoke of love and fear for her future. Her parents spoke often of the worry they had about what would happen to her and whether she would marry.

Mary-Jane could make a sound. It was a guttural sound. The first time she used it her mother jumped with surprise. She was told never to do that again. From that day on she was effectively mute to the world.

She had never had a boyfriend. It was hard to get to know someone who could not speak. Despite all of her problems, she had a fierce determination to make her own way in the world, however limited it was for her.

When her parents died, she was left alone. Her sister, Alice, had married. She wanted Mary-Jane to live with her and her husband. She would be the maiden aunt who cared for the children and generally helped around the house. She would have a home with people who loved her, but it would not be her home.

She set up her own business as a seamstress. Those who tried to cheat her felt her wrath. Her friend would write out the prices on a board and Mary-Jane would, after examining the work that needed fixing, point at the price. There was no bargaining. The price was set.

One day a soldier walked through the doors. He was tall, handsome, and striking in his uniform. Mary-Jane was alone that fateful day. She knew he was the one, but her problems had not gone away. Her natural shyness and inability to talk made their first meeting a disaster.

He assumed that she could understand his questions. When he explained what he needed, she looked at him blankly. She just stood there unable to do anything. He walked out feeling embarrassed and a little silly. She was left feeling frustrated.

It was two weeks before he returned to the workshop. This time he had written a note asking for his trousers to be lengthened. He had bought them in India.

He gave her the note. She shook her head; a tear appeared in the corner of her eye. He said, "Can't read?" She nodded. It was the first time she had ever been ashamed of her affliction. He smiled. He held his trousers up to his waist and pointed at the gap between his highly polished shoes and the hem.

She smiled and took her tape and measured from his waist to where he wanted the hem to be. He never asked the price and she never charged him.

He must have bought a lot of clothes in India, because he would go to her shop at least twice a week. After two months he asked for her hand. He knelt down in the traditional pose; she nodded her acceptance. He met her family and while Mary-Jane held his hand, Alice explained all that he needed to know about her.

"It was when Mary-Jane was about five, she was playing in the yard. She saw her cousin run to meet her. The boy cut across the bull's field. It charged him and continued to gore him until my dad heard what was happening and attacked the bull with a stick.

"Mary-Jane had seen everything. The little boy, named Jimmy, was taken inside the farmhouse and Dad called the doctor. It was too late. He was dead. Mary-Jane had hidden in a corner. She never said another word. My parents tried to get her to talk but gave up. She can hear perfectly well, but they just seemed to give up. I tried to teach her to read, but I'm not very good. Dad didn't think girls needed to read and write."

"So, everyone gave up on her, sorry, dearest." Brendan looked at Mary-Jane and squeezed her hand. "I'm speaking like you're not here."

Mary-Jane leant forward and kissed his cheek. She blushed as her sister smiled at her.

"Mary-Jane was bullied at Sunday school because she couldn't speak. You'll find that she has a real temper when she is being teased. Despite everything, I think she is clever. Her counting is better than mine. After my dad fell ill, we were taken out of school and helped on the farm. I was taught how to look after the animals, and she was taught to be a seamstress. Dad said she was too small to bully the cows into the sheds."

"Please don't worry. I'll look after Mary-Jane and give her whatever she wants or needs."

They married at a small church in his barracks. An army padre officiated at the service. They moved to a flat in

Whitechapel, Brendan was to start a new job as a town crier for the City of London.

Their life was good. Each had their own concerns, worries, and hopes for the future but they knew whatever happened they would be together.

When Brendan lost his job, Mary-Jane secretly took seamstress work without telling him. It helped to ease the financial problems. If Brendan knew about the work, he chose to ignore it. To admit it would prove that he could not look after his wife, the way a man should.

During the period Brendan was working at the coal yard, she would go out in the afternoon and make a dress for a neighbour or take in washing. When he came home there was no evidence of her illicit work.

Her health began to deteriorate, and with it, the work tailed off. Brendan realised she was getting worse her coughing and wheezing started in the morning and only stopped when she went to sleep. This increased the pressure he felt to get her what she needed. The medicines she was prescribed were expensive, even from the pauper hospital.

She sent a letter to her sister, asking for help. Alice was able to send her some money. Mary-Jane was determined that Brendan should not find out about the money. She quietly bought the medicines she needed. She hid them in her sewing box.

The fruit and veg from Borough Market helped a little to keep them fed. Irish stew without the meat was served a couple of times a week.

Mary-Jane noticed a difference in Brendan after he came home later than usual one morning from scavenging at the market. He seemed happier; it did not last. He tried to hide what he was feeling. She tried to elicit a response from him, but he would brush off her obvious distress with a smile and a "Nothing to worry about, dearest".

When the police started to take an interest in Brendan, Mary-Jane was determined to protect him. She had no idea why the police were paying attention to Brendan; could it be the fruit, or perhaps a fight he had? Mary-Jane looked after a cut on his cheek after a scrum at Borough Market.

The only advantage of being considered an idiot was people would ignore you. Mary-Jane's parents had talked in front of her on many occasions. Now the two policemen were discussing Brendan. They totally ignored her. She now knew that Brendan was a suspect in the murder of the town clerk, Mr Hetherington. She had met him once. He seemed stuck up.

After Brendan was arrested and marched out in handcuffs, she knew she had to do something, but the reality was she had no idea how to help him. She waited for him to say something, but he just carried on, unworried. She did notice he was not sleeping properly.

The inevitable happened. Theobald had informed Brendan's boss of his suspicions. Brendan was sacked. Once again, he had to explain to Mary-Jane that he had no job.

Brendan had gone out at midnight to collect coal from his stash in Puddle Dock. Mary-Jane waited for him to return. He was late. It should have been a simple task. When he arrived with the coal, she could tell that something was wrong. After gentle coaching he came clean about Hetherington and Erskine's murders. He also had to tell her about DS Meeks, who he had imprisoned in the coal shed. He was unrepentant but ashamed that he had let her down. She understood. They embraced and cried together.

The following day Brendan was a wreck. He was unable to make the simplest of decisions. Mary-Jane took control of the situation. At midnight, she got dressed and woke him up. She pushed him out of the door, and they walked to Puddle Dock. Brendan showed her where Meeks was tied up. She lit a lamp and peered into Meeks' prison. She showed no empathy for the police officer.

She stood back and pointed at a wall. It was holding up the rest of the building, the shed was directly under it. She pointed at the wall. Brendan knew at once what she was suggesting. He carefully looked over the site and found a sledgehammer. He left it behind the wall. They went home.

The next day she delivered a note to DI Theobald. She was now in control. When Theobald turned up at the designated time, she showed him Meeks, she then disappeared. She waited while the building was hit by Brendan. It was quite quick. The building collapsed onto the police officers. They looked back as the whole façade collapsed into the road. She took Brendan's arm and walked home. They had cocoa before going to bed. That night was never discussed again.

Nine

New Broom

The previous six months had not been good for the O'Carrolls. They were prime suspects in Theobald and Meeks' disappearance. No evidence had been found yet. Brendan was unable to get another job and Mary-Jane was forced to take in washing and sewing.

Brendan was now a fixture in Borough Market. Every night he waited for the leftovers. He had become aggressive in his foraging. Someone told him about the posh hotels in the West End.

For ten hours washing up, it was possible to get a meal and some of the leftovers from the tables. He smartened himself up and waited outside the staff entrance. He had some success. Anything he managed to get was shared with Mary-Jane.

It was the second anniversary of his dismissal from the job of town crier. There were no celebrations in the O'Carroll household. Brendan and Mary-Jane's relationship was as strong as ever. They never mentioned the Puddle Dock incident.

Brendan was forced to appeal to the Friends of Hibernia for relief. He explained about the police informing his boss at the coal yard and how their enquiries had made it difficult to find work.

Mr Treadway was on the panel and explained to his colleagues Theobald's treatment of O'Carroll. They found in his favour and gave him a few shillings to tide him over. They were also able to point him toward a vacancy for a guard in the city. He applied for and got the job. He was in uniform again. He would start as a building guard at the Merchant Marine Insurance company.

***

The police had not forgotten the disappearance of their officers. A new team had taken over the case. DI Jonas Smethwick had transferred in from the Met.

He had been instrumental in the first use of fingerprints to obtain a conviction in nineteen hundred and two. Many officers were still not convinced of this new procedure; many tried to ignore it.

The DI was like a breath of fresh air into a stagnant Wood Street. The city police were known for their deference to privileged suspects; and bad treatment of those at the lower end of society.

He was educated at private school. One of the wave of new schools opening for an emergent middle class. His background was rooted firmly in the 'trade' classes. Jonas joined the Met and worked his way up the ranks. Now in his early forties, he had joined the masons, at the behest of his father.

Politically, he was a progressive with a burning desire for social reform. He believed that poverty caused criminality. However, it had never stopped him from going after criminals; he saw them as bullies.

Jonas was a widower. His wife had died in childbirth. The child had died soon after. From that moment on, Jonas had concentrated on his job. His friends and family had watched as he became more distant. His appearance had drastically changed.

Prior to their deaths, Jonas was a little overweight. He described it as 'contented weight'. Others said he was going to seed. With blue eyes and a generous mouth which had laughter lines, Jonas was always smiling. Just under six feet, he was imposing in his uniform. He was very bright and confident.

His marriage was a success, despite the obvious differences in their backgrounds; Penelope came from a minor aristocratic family in Sligo, Ireland. They were perfect for each other.

She lived in London with her brother; they were orphans. Her parents had died as the result of an attack by Fenians. They were landowners, always guaranteed to be targets in Ireland.

His weight had fallen off of him. His face became leaner. His shirts showed the weight loss. The tell-tale gap between neck and collar was evident to his colleagues.

His hair, almost overnight, had begun to go grey. With his new job he bought a new wardrobe. He slowly regained his old self. His friends were gratified when he tentatively returned to his society friends. He appeared to be more serious, he rarely smiled.

Jonas was specifically given the task of solving the crimes which were collectively known as the 'Puddle Dock Murders'. At the top of the list of suspects was Brendan O'Carroll.

None of the evidence from the bodies of Meeks and Theobald had been kept. Dr Steadman's report on the crime scene had been lost. The case papers that identified Erskine were also lost. Neither Meeks nor Theobald had time to add that the corpse at Blackfriars was Erskine, or what he was doing for Meeks.

The doctor had been quietly retired after an incident involving his drinking.

Jonas interviewed the two officers who had been at Puddle Dock when the bodies of Theobald and Meeks were found. Neither of them mentioned the coal bags. Ominously, no one mentioned Meeks being tied up or that Theobald had his gun in his hand.

Jonas concluded that they were withholding information, but no amount of pressure could get them to change their story.

The leaders of the conspiracy were two long-time constables. Constable Silas Maitland had twenty-five years' service and Constable Gerald Graham had twenty. Both were known to dislike Theobald.

DI Smethwick brought in an experienced detective sergeant named Archie Routledge. He was open to the new ways and showed a good deal of insight.

A new doctor was also engaged by the city police, on recommendation from Jonas. Dr Edward Stapley-Browne was educated at Edinburgh Medical School. He was an aristocrat.

He and Jonas had a met at a crime scene in East London where a family had been butchered by their father. An unlikely friendship had bloomed. Both were advocates of modern policing methods. Both had strong opinions and enjoyed voicing them to each other.

***

Brendan had almost forgotten about the incidents in Puddle Dock. He and Mary-Jane were now reaping the benefits of his job. They had moved to another flat near Fenchurch Street. The premises he was guarding were a few streets away in the Minories.

Brendan was patrolling the yard during the evening when he noticed a police officer standing by the gates of the building.

"Good evening, Officer," Brendan said.

The officer replied, "Stand by me. I have news for you."

Brendan stood by the officer. No one could tell that the officer was whispering to him. He passed over a scrap of paper. The officer saluted him and walked away.

Brendan was frozen to the spot for a moment. The news he had heard was worrying. All the rest of his shift, he was mulling over what he had been told. He had no idea how to deal with this news.

Within a few days, he had been called for an interview

at Wood Street with a DI Smethwick. The DI was totally different to Theobald. No threats, coercion, or trick questions.

Jonas introduced himself and DS Routledge. He continued. "Just a few questions, if I may, to clear up one or two points about the murder of Ernest Hetherington."

Brendan sighed heavily. "Sir, I did not murder him. I told your other officer."

"Of course. I know. But I must clear this case from the roll, otherwise my head is on the line. You understand?"

Brendan nodded. Jonas continued. "Why do you think Detective Inspector Theobald suspected you?" He smiled.

"I worked under Mr Hetherington at the town hall. I was dismissed by the gentleman of the council. He was the one who had to tell me. Many other people were talked to."

Jonas was nodding his head. "Of course. His notes state that your hands were the same size as the bruises on the victim's neck."

"Sir, I was not the only one with big hands. The officer also had them."

Jonas looked at Routledge. "I see. You're not suggesting that the inspector strangled Mr Hetherington?" Brendan said nothing.

Jonas continued. "Come, come, Sergeant Major. May I call you by your rank? You're not suggesting a detective murdered him. Why?"

Brendan just said very quietly, "It seems to me, sir, that there is as much evidence against him as me."

"Interesting," Jonas replied. "What do you think, Sergeant Routledge?"

"Well, sir, it's certainly a new line of investigation. I can't help thinking that it's unlikely. But we can consider it, sir."

"Thank you, Mr O'Carroll. I may have to see you again."

Brendan began to stand. "Oh, one last question…" Jonas waited while Brendan sat down again.

"Will your wife be able to give you an alibi for September the twelfth?"

Brendan visibly tensed. "My wife knows nothing of Mr Hetherington. She is mute."

"Will she give me a written statement?" Jonas asked.

"My wife cannot read or write. You can question me all you like. Stay away from Mary-Jane." The threat was clear.

Jonas did not answer or react. Instead, he brought the interview to an end. Brendan left Wood Street police station and went to work.

"Well, Archie, what do you think?"

The DS thought for a minute. "It'll need a good deal more evidence to break him, sir. Do you think we should bring his wife in for questioning?"

"No, she'll give us nothing. Maybe we can put pressure on her to break him."

"I'm worried that he seemed to know where your line of questioning was going," Routledge said.

"Ah, you noticed that," Jonas replied. "It's almost as if he knew what I was going to ask."

Both detectives were quiet for a moment. "You know, Theobald claimed that someone in the station was trying to sabotage his case against O'Carroll," Jonas said.

"I think we'll have to be little more discreet when

discussing this case. I've no intention of it being ruined by friends of O'Carroll."

"We need to find that missing evidence. Then get Dr Stapley-Browne to go over it," Routledge said.

"I agree. Bring in two of the newest constables. We'll get them to go through every case file, cupboard and hiding place in the station. After that we can interrogate those officers most likely to help O'Carroll. If necessary, we'll search their homes."

Ten

Lost Evidence?

The two constables were told not to speak to anyone about what they were doing. They were told to refer any enquiries to DI Smethwick. They worked their way through all the files and looked into areas not disturbed since the building was constructed.

Jonas finally had to admit defeat. The records were nowhere in the station. Jonas and Routledge then investigated the backgrounds of the officers in the station. Two names came up time and again.

PCs Maitland and Graham were both associated with the 'Friends of Hibernia'. Both were voluntary welfare officers. Over the years several suspects had been given legal representation from the FoH. It was not illegal, but it had stymied senior officers in their quest for a conviction.

Jonas knew about the FoH. It had suspected links with the troubles in Ireland. It was funded by shadowy figures in the United States. Jonas served an intention to interview PC Maitland.

Jonas and Routledge waited in the interrogation room. Maitland and Jonathan Treadway entered. They introduced themselves.

Jonas started. "PC Maitland…You do not have to say anything…" When the caution was given, Mr Treadway asked why his client was there.

"I am investigating the loss of evidence in the cases of the murder of Ernest Hetherington and an unidentified body found at Blackfriars Bridge," Jonas replied.

"And you believe my client can help you; you suspect him of losing this evidence or perhaps stealing it?"

"I do," replied Jonas.

"Detective Inspector Smethwick, I have advised my client not to say anything. If you have evidence of any crime, please arrest him or we will be leaving this interview."

Jonas and Routledge sat in silence.

"I thought so," said Treadway. "We are leaving." Maitland and Treadway left the interview room. The same procedure was enacted with PC Graham.

The two detectives sat in the interrogation room. Routledge was the first to speak, "Sir, where do we go from here? I've no doubt O'Carroll is the murderer, and that Maitland and Graham are protecting him. Without a breakthrough, we're stumped."

Jonas thought for a moment. "We know that the two constables were on the Theobald and Meeks' incident scene first. They would have had time to arrange the evidence or remove it, yes?"

Routledge replied, "Yes, sir. It was at least a half-hour before other officers arrived."

"So, Maitland and Graham had more than enough time to clean the scene up. We know that Theobald was armed. He had signed ammunition out the night he left Wood Street. Why would he need a gun?"

"Sir, it's just struck me that we may not need the evidence from Maitland and Graham."

"Please explain."

"Who alerted the police to the discovery of the bodies? Someone was there before the officers. They may have a different take on how the scene looked."

"Excellent, Archie, we need to interview the workers at the site. They may be able to give us a clearer idea of the incident scene."

Sergeant Routledge returned to Puddle Dock, where a new building was being erected. After some enquiries, he managed to get the name of the demolition company. He wasted no time and went to their registered offices in Hackney.

Routledge sat opposite the owner, James Molloy, in a makeshift canteen. It was the only free area. Molloy was owner and worker. It was a small company which relied on recruiting from street corners in the borough. All those employed were day workers.

The DS started by confirming that Molloy had the contract to demolish the old warehouse.

"I'd like to take you back to the day your crew found the bodies. Can you recall that incident?"

"Of course, sir. Tim, Tim Grieves, my ganger-man, told me that a couple of bodies were squashed under the rubble."

"Can you recall who actually found them? Was it Tim?"

"No, I think it was Murphy and Cleats."

"First names?"

"George Murphy and Martin Cleats."

"Do they still work for you?"

"No. Murphy went home to Dublin. And I dismissed Cleats for drinking on the job."

"I don't suppose you have their addresses?"

"Sorry, I'd pick them up outside the Shipwright Arms each morning. I know that Murphy suddenly came into money. He turned down at least three month's work on the demolition. I've seen Cleats hanging around trying to get a day's work. But he's been a drunk for a long time. No one wants him on their site. He's a danger to himself and everyone he works with."

"Thanks, Mr Molloy. Could I have a word with Tim?"

"He's out looking for new men for a small job I've got for next week. I can get him to come and see you if you like?"

"Do you have his address?"

"Sir, I'd rather not. He lives in an area that's controlled by the boyos. If they saw him talking to a stranger, a policeman, they'd certainly make his life a misery. Do you understand, sir?"

DS Routledge smiled. "Okay. Make sure he comes to Wood Street and asks for me."

"Sir, would it be possible to meet somewhere else? Wood Street is known for its links; if you get my meaning."

"Fleet Street, Printers' Arms, nine tomorrow night. Tell him not to be late, or I'll come and find him."

"You're a gentleman, sir. I'll tell him."

"Oh, one thing more, do not discuss what we've talked about to anyone else. Even if they are dressed in police uniform. Do you understand?"

"Of course, sir. I understand. I want no trouble from anyone."

Later at Wood Street, DS Routledge started to tell DI Smethwick about his conversation. The DI held his hand up. Routledge stopped talking.

Smethwick opened his office door very quickly. "May I help you constable?" he said to PC Maitland.

"No sir, I just dropped my papers." Maitland was on his knees picking up a file of papers.

Smethwick waited until Maitland had collected the papers and went away. As he closed the door, he said, "We can't talk here. I'm not sure what he heard, but we will adjourn to somewhere more discreet."

As DI Smethwick and DS Routledge left the station, Maitland and PC Graham watched them intently.

The 'Pie House' was situated by Shoreditch municipal baths. The establishment catered for those gentlemen who needed a little privacy. Smethwick had been introduced to the proprietor, Mr Rossi, an Italian émigré who had fled from Rome. No one knew why or cared.

"Ah, Inspector, so pleased to see you again. Your usual table?"

"Thank you, Guido. This is Mr Routledge, a colleague, may I sign him in?"

"Of course, of course."

Routledge was led to the ornate counter where he signed in and wrote his profession, civil servant.

Routledge was feeling a little lost, as they were led to a table in a corner. Smethwick picked up on his discomfiture.

"Relax, Archie. We can talk in total privacy. And, of course, the pies are on me." He laughed.

Guido supervised as the pies, potatoes and lashings of gravy were brought to their table.

They talked quietly about the case as they tucked into the repast. Smethwick was concerned when Routledge recounted what Molloy had intimated about Wood Street and the 'boyos'.

"If that's true, we cannot rely on getting the necessary help in cracking this case. We must sound out those at Wood Street we can trust. They cannot all be associated with the FoH," Smethwick said.

Routledge told him of his planned meeting with Tim Grieves the next night. Smethwick told him to sign out a firearm, just in case it was a set up.

DS Routledge sat in a corner facing the main door of the Printers' Arms. Tim Grieves was a tall man, with a strong physique. Years of wielding a sledgehammer had built him up.

Routledge nodded at him. Tim walked slowly toward the detective. It was obvious he was nervous. He sat down and removed his cap. His hair was receding and what was left had a deep ginger hue with flecks of grey at the temples. He looked about forty.

Routledge looked at the barmen and nodded. A pint of Guinness was brought for Grieves. He took a sip of the drink, pulled a face, and pushed it to one side.

"Not a Guinness man then?" Routledge smiled.

Grieves answered in a strong London accent, "Listen, guvnor, I don't want no trouble. If someone sees me talking to a 'cozzer', I'll end up in the Thames with me throat slit."

"No one's going to know we talked. I just want to know what you saw when Murphy and Cleats told you about the bodies in the rubble."

Grieves kept on looking around the pub. Routledge slammed the table with his fist. Grieves jumped with the shock.

"Concentrate. Or I'll take you in to Wood Street nick. I don't think you'll like that."

After he had settled down, Grieves began to say what had happened.

"Murphy called me over and pointed to a leg poking out of the rubble. Cleats was removing the bricks and wood and exposed two bodies. One was dressed like a toff. There was a cane nearby. In his hand was a pistol. Behind him was a smaller man. His hands and feet were tied up. He was gagged. A blindfold was around what was left of his face."

"What did you do next?"

"I went to call for a copper. I left Murphy and Cleats with the bodies. When I got back, I noticed that the bodies had been rifled. Murphy and Cleats were going through a few items. They were sharing out some money. They offered me a couple of pounds. I refused. Murphy then pointed a pistol at me and said that If I told anyone that they had robbed the bodies, they would kill me."

"Describe the bodies. Anything you can remember."

"The tied-up one had a lot of coal dust on him. He was surrounded by coal bags. The toff was laying across him. It looked like the whole structure had fallen on the bodies. A door was laying on top of the toff. It was moved to one side by either Murphy or Cleats. I noticed holes in the door. It looked like bullet holes to me. I'm ex-army."

"Coal dust, are you absolutely sure?"

"Yes, some of the other guys started to collect it in bags and hide it to take home."

"When did the police turn up?"

"It was about three-quarters of an hour later. Two PCs. They spoke to Murphy and Cleats. I thought they knew them."

"Are you saying that the officers knew Murphy and Cleats?"

"I've no doubt. They shook hands with them. I'm not sure, but I think a few trinkets were passed over."

"What happened next?"

"Murphy and Cleats got their clothes and walked off the site. I was told to keep everyone away from the bodies. They didn't ask me about the pockets that were turned out, and I didn't offer any information."

"What happened next?"

"I saw the two officers moving the bodies away from the coal bags. After ten minutes, they were joined by another two constables. By the time I looked again, the bodies were placed in a different area and the gag, blindfold and ties were removed."

"They had rearranged the crime scene. Is that what you are saying?"

"It certainly looked that way."

"Why didn't you say something?"

"A big copper, slight Irish accent, warned me off. I was to forget what I saw, or else. He knew where I lived. He said I would be watched to make sure I was a good boy."

"So, you kept quiet."

"Listen, I live in area that is full of Irish guys. My wife is Irish. They wouldn't think twice about shooting me if they thought I was a grass. I keep my nose clean. I don't get involved in thievery or politics. All I want is to provide for my wife and kids. Can you understand that?"

"You'll need to make a statement."

"No way, as soon as I do that, I'm dead. My brother-in-law is associated with several scary guys. He doesn't trust me, anyway. The only reason I'm allowed to move freely around that area is because of the wife. No, you can lock me up if you want, at least I'll be alive; and the wife and kids will be looked after."

Despite all the threats DS Routledge tried, Grieves was adamant. Routledge allowed him to leave. He could always arrest him later, if necessary.

Routledge briefed Smethwick on what Grieves had said. They had a credible tale that would convict O'Carroll of murder, Maitland, and Graham of tampering with evidence, Murphy, and Cleats of robbery and lastly, all of them for conspiracy.

The frustrating part was the lack of corroboration. Knowing that someone had committed a crime was not the same as having the evidence to prove it.

Eleven

The Friends of Hibernia

Maitland had not been idle since his interview with Smethwick. Using his unofficial army of colleagues and informers, he had organised an almost faultless spy network to follow the DI and DS.

Maitland and Graham knew that they had interviewed Molloy and Grieves. They guessed that Grieves had told the detectives about Murphy and Cleats.

Murphy was safely away in Dublin. Cleats and Grieves were a problem. Grieves was English, ex-army and had no sympathy for 'the cause'. He would have to be removed before he made a statement about what he saw.

Cleats was a habitual drunk. He would not last more than a day before telling all. Maitland knew of someone who could be persuaded to do him a favour.

Maitland and Graham agreed on the next steps. Grieves would have an unfortunate accident while on site. Cleats would drink himself to death next week. Satisfied, they put the plan into action.

DI Smethwick had tasked Routledge with finding Cleats. It was clear to the detectives that they were being watched. In many instances, during interviews which they had attended, they saw constables that were off their beat, standing nearby.

Smethwick decided to fight back. The senior sergeant at Wood Street was an Englishman who had been stationed in Ireland, when he was an RSM in the army. He was known to dislike and distrust the Friends of Hibernia and those who associated with it.

Sergeant Smith knew that PC Maitland was likely to be promoted in his place when he retired in two years' time. Maitland had passed the exams and had fended off any attempts to promote him away from Wood Street.

Smith was getting ready to go on duty when there was a knock on his door. He opened it and saw DI Smethwick standing there with DS Routledge. He saluted the senior officer. He invited them in.

"Sergeant Smith, I need your help," Smethwick said as he walked in. "What do you know of the Friends of Hibernia?"

"Has been the bane of my life for the last twenty years. They've corrupted young officers and sabotaged cases against Fenians. Wood Street is riddled with their corruption, sir."

Smethwick smiled. "I take it you do not like them?"

"Sir, I've seen so many good officers either forced out or deliberately shunted down dead ends. Innocent people found guilty and the guilty found innocent. They are a dark force within the police service, sir."

"Would you be willing to help me eradicate their evil, Sergeant?"

"Others have tried before, sir. Your predecessor tried. He ended up dead. He knew that they engaged in criminality but was stymied at every turn."

Smith thought for a moment. "Sir, I have two years left before I leave the service. I know that one of the biggest troublemakers will take my position. The FoH will be able to sabotage the police on a different scale. Yes, I will help you."

Smethwick held his hand out and shook Smith's hand. "I knew I could rely on you, Sergeant."

"You know you and Sergeant Routledge are being watched?"

"I guessed as much," said Smethwick.

"I caught a young constable off his beat. His excuse was that PC Graham had told him that the senior PCs were worried that the detectives were in danger, and the constable would be a backup if anything happened. He was to report your whereabouts only to Maitland or Graham. I spoke to Maitland and his excuse was he didn't want another detective being killed from his station. Said it was bad for all our promotions. Of course, he's lying."

"Thank you, Sergeant Smith. Do you know if they are still watching us?" Smethwick enquired.

"I warned off the constables. But knowing Maitland, he'll get some villain to follow you rather than miss out on decent intelligence."

DS Routledge pondered whether the FoH knew about his questioning Grieves.

"Sir, based on this information, I wonder if it would be safer to arrest Tim Grieves. We can put him in another station while we try to get a statement."

"I see, you think his life is at risk?"

"I do, sir. He's the only evidence we have so far. Murphy's safely ensconced in Ireland. No one knows where Cleats is. He seems to have vanished."

"Okay, pick him up. Do you know any trustworthy men in Wood Street, Sergeant Smith?"

"Yes, sir, I've a couple of lads that I trust completely."

"Good, Archie, take the sergeant's lads and get Grieves. I'll have a word with a colleague across the Thames. No one will suspect Grieves is at Tower Bridge police station."

Tim Grieves was supervising the demolition of a warehouse on the Wapping riverfront. He was watching a newcomer intently. He was not sure that the man was experienced enough to undertake the high work. But he was overruled by his boss.

The man was two storeys up, balancing on a brick wall that was perhaps four or five bricks wide. He was gingerly removing bricks with his pick. He worked slowly and moved forward at a steady pace.

Grieves watched for a few minutes then, satisfied that he was better than he first hoped, walked to the site office.

The man came to a difficult corner. Grieves wanted to see how he would deal with it. There was a right way of removing corners. The man picked away at the top and removed the bricks slowly. He deftly moved to the opposite wall. The corner stack was standing alone.

Tim Grieves was always careful while on site. He avoided standing anywhere near where a wall could collapse or near the brick piles.

He noticed a group of men standing around a fire

warming themselves. He strode across to them, "What the hell do you think you're doing? I'm not paying you to stand around."

The men quickly ran to their designated jobs. Grieves was fuming. The job was already late. The boss was giving him grief. He turned. Returning to the office he heard a shout, looked up and saw the corner stack falling. He tried to run but tripped.

He was covered by the stack of bricks. He died instantly. The newcomer was sitting astride the brick wall in front of the rest of the corner stack. He showed no emotion as many workers tried to dig Grieves out.

It was just another accident in an industry noted for its high death rate. The constable who visited the site noted that it was an accident. Mr Grieves was standing near a high-risk area. PC Graham closed his notebook. The body was removed, and the demolition continued.

Sergeant Routledge saw the body in the morgue. He was not pleased that he had been outwitted again.

***

Brendan O'Carroll was patrolling around his building. He saw PC Maitland waiting by the entrance.

"Good evening, Officer."

"We need to talk." Maitland was terse in his speech.

Brendan opened the door and led the PC into a small office. It had two chairs and a table. It had an electric light, which Brendan flicked on.

"How have you been, Mr O'Carroll?"

"Fine, sir, thank you."

"Good, this is a very good job. You're lucky to have a job here. Secure work and good wages. Another few years and you could retire. How's Mrs O'Carroll?"

"She's a little poorly, but I'm sure she'll get better; with the right medicines."

"That's good. Expensive, are they? I mean the medicines."

"Yes, sir, I can't tell you how much I appreciate your help and, of course, the Friends."

Maitland was smiling. "Yes, a nice little job. Speaking of the Friends, I wonder if you would be willing to lend a hand. We've a problem that needs your particular skill set?"

"Of course, what can I do to help?"

***

Smethwick and Routledge were seated in the pie house, Guido was standing over them pointing out the day's specials. They settled on an oyster and beef pie, split between them.

Smethwick waited until Guido had left. "So, Grieves was killed. Accident, the report said. What do you think, Sergeant?"

"It is a dangerous occupation, demolition. However, it's too much of a coincidence. And the reporting officer was PC Graham."

"My feelings exactly. Have we found Cleats yet?"

"No, sir, he seems to have vanished. I've got a few of my narks trying to find him. Is there any chance we can get Murphy picked up and brought back?"

"I've already asked. It seems it's too expensive, unless I

can get real evidence against him the boss will not sanction it."

The detectives sat quietly pondering what to do next. They left the pie house, feeling very down.

Twelve
Special Irish Branch

B rendan O'Carroll finished his shift and walked toward his home. Mary-Jane had a meal waiting for him. He sat by the fire and drank a mug of tea. Mary-Jane brought him a newspaper. He smiled. "Not today, dearest, I've a lot to think about."

She gently touched his arm. He knew he would have to tell her.

"The Friends of Hibernia have asked me to help them. It's not nice. I'd hoped I could forget what I'd done. If I refuse, I'll end up swinging, or likely lose my job and be on the streets again."

Mary-Jane held his hand and smiled. She nodded her head in agreement.

"So, I'm to help them? Are you sure, dearest?"

***

DI Smethwick sat in his office in Wood Street. The door was closed. He viewed the outside as hostile territory. He read his notes on the Puddle Dock murder and the associated murders of Theobald and Meeks.

DS Routledge knocked on the door, "You wanted me, sir?"

"Yes, Archie, get in here. I need your input."

"Read this." He passed over a file.

Archie read the file while Jonas waited patiently. DS Routledge finished reading and gave it back.

"Well, what do you think?"

"Sir, the unidentified man and now Grieves, is linked to the original murder of Hetherington, I have no doubt. I wonder why a seemingly opportunistic murder, with a questionable motive, should escalate into a conspiracy involving the Friends of Hibernia. What possible motive was there for the FoH to involve themselves? That they are protecting O'Carroll is obvious. But why?"

Smethwick agreed with Archie. "Okay, let's do this logically."

He took a piece of paper and wrote, 'Hetherington, Murphy, Cleats, Theobald, Meeks, coal dust, O'Carroll, firearm, Grieves, FoH.'

He crossed out all of those who had died. He was left with Murphy, Cleats, O'Carroll, coal dust, firearm and FoH.

He sat back in his chair. O'Carroll and the coal dust were underlined. He annotated this, 'number one'. Murphy, Cleats, and the firearm were similarly underlined. He put a question mark against this and annotated it, 'number two'.

The FoH was isolated. They were number three. As he stared at the jottings, he said to Archie, "Cleats is a drunk. He's no use to anyone. He's a loose end. I would remove him, before he could talk. Murphy seems to be the key player. Would he have Theobald's gun? It would be useful in Dublin. Firearms are scarce since the army clamped down on the Fenian troublemakers. Was Murphy the instigator of the conspiracy of the detectives' murder? We need Murphy."

"So where do we start? His last sighting was in Dublin. Can we get him back?"

"I'll try. I can only ask. I have another idea. It is a longshot. A colleague from my early days in the Met may be able to help," Jonas said.

Since Sergeant Smith had spoken to Maitland and Graham, their unofficial use of naïve police constables to follow Smethwick and Routledge had stopped.

It was likely that they were using other means to trail the detectives.

Ordinarily, detectives had to leave their colleagues with a note as to where they were going or who they were interviewing. This was held on the station sergeant's desk. Any officer could look at it. Smith now kept it in a locked drawer. Anyone wanting to read it had to go through him. Effectively, Smethwick and Routledge's whereabouts became confidential.

***

Guido welcomed Smethwick to the pie house. Routledge was away trying to find Cleats. Jonas Smethwick settled in his favourite corner. The table was laid for two.

Guido took the coat of a visitor who had stopped at the desk. He was led over to Smethwick's table.

"Jonas, how nice to see you after all this time." The stranger held his hand out. Jonas took it and smiled.

"Arthur, please sit down." They chatted quietly until Guido and the waiter had delivered the food.

"How's Jane?" Jonas enquired.

"Fine. We just had our second child. A boy, quite a handful."

"Oh, congratulations, you must allow me to send you a piece of silver for the boy. A belated Christening present."

"Thank you, Jane would appreciate that." He paused while the waiter poured out the wine.

"I was sorry to hear of Penelope. I wanted to contact you, but…you know, the job."

"Thank you for your condolences. She was far too young to die."

Jonas picked the wine glass up and took a sip. "I never really understood how lonely it could get without her."

Guido interrupted the solemn moment, "Everything to your satisfaction, gentlemen?" He went away happy.

"So, what can I do for you, Jonas?"

"Was it so obvious?" he replied.

"Well, I haven't seen you since you left to become a detective."

"I have a case. Conspiracy, murder, the usual." He laughed. "However, it's trespassing into your area."

"I see. Perhaps you should enlighten me."

Smethwick spent the next hour explaining the case and his theories about the involvement of the Friends of Hibernia. Arthur said nothing and listened intently.

"So, you see, without finding Murphy, I'm stumped," Jonas finished.

Arthur looked intently at Jonas.

"I know of the FoH. On the surface a respectable group of charitable-minded individuals, intent on helping the Irish community. Most of them are decent law-abiding people, however, there are a few of its leaders who are involved in organising terror attacks in Ireland and England. They collect money for guns and train volunteers in the wilds of Connemara. If, as you suspect, Murphy is involved, it will not be too difficult to find out about him. Leave it with me."

The Honourable Arthur Middleton was the second son of an aristocratic family. The family seat was situated in Offaly, in Ireland. He was smaller than Jonas. He had the build of a sportsman; he was superb rugby player, capped once for England. His nose was misshaped as a result of being hit in a game. When he stared at a suspect, they knew he meant business. To his friends, he was charming, educated and kind.

After university, he enlisted in the military; very boring. He had joined the diplomatic service after leaving the army. A few postings around the world had followed. In truth, he found the service to be boring too.

After a less than spectacular period managing his older brother's estate, he had been invited to join a new organisation protecting England's interests in Ireland; The Special Irish Branch (SIB). It was all that he had hoped for.

All its senior staff were from the 'right' background. Everyone was university educated and all could mix in the right circles. Arthur had met Jonas through his first case, tracking down an Irish saboteur near the docks at Chatham.

Jonas was a lowly constable who had arrested the suspect for theft. The SIB then took over the case and managed to persuade the man to work for them.

Jonas' work on the case was noted and it was the start of his rise through the ranks of the police service.

After a thorough look through the archives, Arthur had managed to identify George Murphy as George Collins, a man wanted by the British authorities in Ireland. Martin Cleats was also wanted for gunrunning.

Arthur made copious notes of their background and friends, where they lived and other aliases. He telegraphed the SIB office in Dublin and told them that George Collins was using the name George Murphy and was believed to be in Dublin.

DI Smethwick received the intelligence from Arthur by courier. No one other than Smethwick and DS Routledge were privy to the information gleaned from the SIB.

They now had an old address for Martin Cleats. Smethwick left Wood Street first. Followed by DS Routledge ten minutes later. They intended to meet up in the afternoon. Anyone trailing them would have a wasted day.

DI Smethwick lost his tail reasonably quickly. He hailed a cab and was lost in the rush of city traffic. Routledge used his knowledge of the streets. He was a fit man and easily left his shadow far behind.

The detectives met up in Tanner Street, on the south side of the river. They could see a block of flats opposite a waste ground. Lots of children were playing. This was a problem. If they were noticed, the children would follow them shouting, 'coppers-on-the-beat'. Everyone would know that they were hunting for someone.

Smethwick decided that they should split up. Routledge headed toward the children. He deliberately led them away from Cleats' address. The children were shouting aloud as they followed him.

Smethwick quietly walked toward the flats. He entered without being seen. He ran up the stairs to the top floor. Number nine was like all the other flats. It was dark; there was no light on the landing. The door was painted in a dull colour. The paint was flaking. A string was hanging through the middle of the door.

Smethwick gently pulled on the large knot at its end. The door latch was opened on the other side. He pushed the door open. A smell of stale tobacco and sick assailed his senses.

A gas burner was giving off a weak light. The fireplace was cold. A few embers still glowed. He walked in and saw several beer bottles strewn across the floor.

The furniture was broken and stained. The flat consisted of the one room. Smethwick allowed himself a little sympathy for the man he saw, head down toward the floor over a bucket, from where a rancid smell was emanating.

The body did not move. Smethwick thought that he was dead. He moved forward. At that moment, the man coughed and loudly broke wind. Smethwick moved back a little, as the odour enveloped the room.

He put a handkerchief to his nose and mouth. He waited. The man remained in a drunken stupor.

Smethwick reached into his pocket and removed the

cuffs he was carrying. He had Cleats handcuffed before he was even aware of the restraints.

Routledge had lost the children, or they had become bored of following him. He walked into the flat and started to retch. He quickly walked over to the window and tried to open it; it was nailed shut.

Routledge's face was turning pale. He felt sick and quickly volunteered to get a cab. Smethwick laughed. "Best get a Black Maria, I don't think a cabbie would like this pile of ordure in his cab."

Cleats was transported to Tower Bridge police station. He was still unconscious when he was put in a cell. Smethwick gave instructions that the prisoner was to be isolated and only he or Routledge were to be told when he woke up.

Thirteen
The Raid

Smethwick decided to have Cleats arrested by Arthur Middleton. He hoped that this ruse would keep Cleats safe from any accidents or FoH interference.

The plan worked well. Cleats was taken from Tower Bridge police station as soon as he woke up. He was now housed in a holding cell in Paddington.

A SIB sergeant took the lead interviewing Cleats after he had sobered up and been cleaned. The sergeant made it quite clear that he did not like Cleats, or his politics. He also inferred that Cleats would be lucky to get out alive.

With a combination of astute questioning and blatant threats, the sergeant persuaded the suspect to reveal information about the FoH in London and Ireland.

The sergeant left the interrogation room and as he passed Smethwick and Routledge, he said, "All yours, sir."

Smethwick and Routledge entered the room and stood over the prisoner.

"Listen, sir," Cleats began, "I've told you everything I know. Please allow me to rest. I don't feel well." He spoke in a whisper. His accent was clearly a mixture of London and rural Irish.

The detectives sat down opposite him. Routledge started the questioning.

"We're investigating the murder of two police officers. I believe you may have information useful in the case. We want to talk to you about the bodies you found at Puddle Dock."

"I know nothing about bodies."

Routledge looked at Cleats then spoke to Smethwick. "Sir, I wonder if you could leave the room for about five minutes?"

Smethwick understood. "Of course, Sergeant. I'll just have a cigarette." As he left, he took the constable with him. Cleats and the DS were alone now.

DS Routledge stood up and removed his jacket. He then unbuttoned his shirt sleeves and slowly rolled them up. He said nothing while he did this. He kept his eyes firmly on Cleats.

After an hour, Routledge appeared from the room. He was unrolling his sleeves and tidying himself.

"Well?" Smethwick asked.

"He opened up, sir. He's willing to sign a statement. I think it's enough to suspend Maitland and Graham."

"You didn't touch him?"

"No, sir, he was ready to talk as soon as I meant business."

"Well, done, Sergeant. Get his statement. I'll go through

it, and we can then clear up any inconsistencies before he's transported to Dublin to answer the gunrunning charges."

***

Brendan O'Carroll was waiting at the rendezvous point in Waterloo station. He was concerned that he would have to kill someone else before the night was out. However, after he was met by the leader, he realised that his part was not as an assassin.

He was given a uniform and told to change into it in the gentlemen's toilets on the station concourse. It was a sergeant major's uniform, in an infantry unit. He would have preferred his old unit. But his mild protestations were slapped down by the leader of the group.

The group left the station and walked down to the Cut. An army lorry was waiting for them. Brendan sat in the front by the driver, while the others got into the back. They drove off toward Woolwich. As they reached the Woolwich Dockyard, they drove to a warehouse on the riverfront. Most of the dockyard was used by the Woolwich Arsenal to store goods of every kind. What was not public knowledge was that arms were stored there before being shipped to the empire.

Brendan and two civilians approached the guard. He came to attention as he saw the sergeant major. They entered the office. As they did, the two civilians disarmed the startled army clerks. The guard was called in and he was disarmed and tied up.

They took the clerk's keys and opened the warehouse. The lorry was backed up to the loading bay. Brendan saw for the first time that there were three others in the lorry. They started to lift various arms and ammunition into its rear. Brendan stood outside the entrance and watched as other workers and soldiers went about their business.

Brendan pulled up a squaddie who had dirty boots. He was in his element now. After half an hour, the lorry was full. The others scrambled into the back and Brendan returned to the passenger seat. No one interfered with them.

They drove to a warehouse in Bermondsey and unloaded the vehicle. Brendan changed into his civilian clothes; he was given a crisp new five-pound note for his troubles. Liam Cartney gave each of the other men a five-pound note.

Brendan noticed that the man had a wad of notes. Liam saw Brendan looking at him. He quickly put the money away and turned his back.

Brendan realised it was time to go. He walked home across Tower Bridge.

The first editions of the newspapers the next day had the audacious robbery on the front page. The suspects were identified as Fenians. The later editions hinted that it could have been undertaken by German spies.

Maitland and Graham had heard about the arrest of Cleats. However, they had failed to track him down. The FoH solicitor, Mr Treadway, had been unable to find out where he was being held.

All of Treadway's complaints were dismissed by senior officers. A new phrase was heard, that of, 'In the interests of National Security'.

Maitland and Graham were tipped off that they were to be suspended and arrested by DI Smethwick. They both disappeared from their homes. A warrant for their arrest was issued by the City of London Police.

DI Smethwick was in his office with DS Routledge. They were working out their strategy for the arrest of Maitland and Graham. There was a knock at the door, a constable came in, "Sir, I have an officer from the special branch, he would like to see you."

"Of course, show him in."

Arthur Middleton walked in. "Good morning, Jonas. Not disturbing you, am I?"

"Of course not. Come in, take a seat." Routledge gave his seat up.

"This is DS Routledge."

"Good morning, sir." Routledge began to leave the room.

"Could your sergeant stay? I believe his insight could be useful to my problem."

"Sergeant, find a seat." Smethwick nodded.

"I take it you've heard about the dockyard robbery?" Arthur began. Both Smethwick and Routledge agreed.

"I've been asked to investigate. There were three men, an army lorry and driver, who the guard saw. We believe that the lorry also had at least two more men to load the arms. The guard gave a good description of the man in charge. He was someone used to giving orders. He ordered the others in a quiet manner. The guard thought he had a slight accent, maybe Irish.

"They used an NCO to gain access. The man was dressed as a warrant officer. The guard was sure that the man had the rank. He was sure of himself. He knew the procedures and was confident in his manner. The guard heard him tearing a strip of a soldier for slovenliness. It was his description that brought me here. Tall, over six feet, large moustache, reddish. Well-built, bear-like man. Remind you of anyone?"

Smethwick and Routledge both spoke at the same time, "Brendan O'Carroll!"

"That's my feeling," Arthur replied.

"But why would he involve himself in an arms robbery?" Routledge asked.

"If we ignore the murder of Hetherington, O'Carroll was, up to that point, a law-abiding person. Clean military record and well respected in his role as town crier."

Smethwick thought for a moment. "Blackmail" it's the only possible explanation."

"That's what I thought," Arthur agreed.

"I thought the robbery was down to German spies?" Routledge mused.

Arthur answered, "This information must not leave this room. We believe that the FoH and German sympathisers have allied themselves to undertake an attack against England's interests. We do not know what the target is, at present."

"I take it you would like us to arrest O'Carroll for the robbery?"

"Special branch would be eternally grateful. We could do it ourselves, but it would have to involve the Met in Woolwich. And that entails a good deal of collaboration and, I'm afraid, in-fighting."

"I see," said Smethwick. "You said, 'special branch'? Have you changed your name?"

"We have dropped the 'Irish' part of the name. We still look after Irish problems, but we have a new enemy on the horizon, Germany. We are to be expanded within the Metropolitan police service. It's causing some discord. Hence my request."

Smethwick smiled. "I'll have to let Woolwich know of my interest."

"That's fine. You are the city police. No one likes you." They all laughed.

"In truth, you do not have to worry about Woolwich. The robbery happened on crown property, of crown munitions. It is a special branch investigation. But we do need your expertise. Your knowledge of the main suspects would be invaluable."

Brendan O'Carroll was arrested at home the following day and taken to Woolwich police station.

Fourteen

Brendan Cornered

"So, Mr O'Carroll, you've expanded your crimes somewhat. Murder, robbery, and treason. Looks like you'll be hanged very soon." Smethwick did not look away from Brendan.

"I know nothing of murder or robbery and I would never commit treason. You're just trying to get me for anything. You couldn't prove murder, so now you're intent on putting me away for crimes I haven't done."

"I have a witness. Sergeant, bring him in." Brendan looked at the door as the guard walked in. "Do you recognise anyone in this room, Private?"

"Yes, sir, that's the man that was dressed as a WO1."

"Thank you, Private," Smethwick said. He turned back to O'Carroll.

"My colleagues in the special branch are determined to charge you with treason. You'll hang as a traitor. Your regiment will expunge you from their records. Your medals will be taken from you. Your friends in the FoH will distance themselves from you. Your wife will be put on the street. How long do you think before Mary-Jane deteriorates and is found dead on a bench, perhaps in Puddle Dock?"

Brendan O'Carroll knew that he was caught. He remained quiet for some time. Smethwick waited for him to speak. The tension in the room could be felt.

"What do you what to know?"

"Let's concentrate on the robbery. Who else was with you?"

"I don't know their names. I never saw them before."

"That's not what I want to hear. Sergeant, arrest him for treason. Take him back to the cells." Smethwick stood up and walked to the door.

Routledge was cuffing O'Carroll.

"It's the truth. I swear on Mary-Jane's life."

Smethwick nodded to the DS and said, "I want to know everything you know. Do not miss out a single point. I swear, if you lie to me, you'll spend your last hours in the Tower of London. A fitting place for traitors."

"I was approached by a police officer one night while I was on patrol."

"Name?" Smethwick was tense.

"PC Maitland, he's a friend. He said he knew about my past. He said I was helped by the FoH, and now they needed my help. I had no choice. I had to agree."

"So, what did he mean, 'your past'?"

"The trouble with the Hetherington case."

"He knew you had murdered Hetherington?" Smethwick was waiting for O'Carroll's admission.

"I did not murder Mr Hetherington," Brendan said in a quiet voice.

Smethwick was annoyed that he had not been able to trick O'Carroll.

"All right, he suspected you, is that fair?"

Brendan said, "Yes."

"So why did you agree to help him if you knew you were innocent?" Routledge asked.

"Because they had helped me with a solicitor, welfare payments and a job. I was indebted to them. It was a debt of honour. I couldn't refuse. PC Maitland gave me a meeting place and date. He didn't say what the job was. I turned up at Waterloo station and was met by a man I've never seen before. He gave me a uniform and I dressed in it. I followed him to an army vehicle. I heard others in the back but didn't see them until we went into the clerk's office."

"I need descriptions."

"I only really saw the main man. He had an Irish accent. Sounded like a Dubliner. He was about five feet ten, stocky, greying hair. He knew what he was doing. Used to commanding men, I would have thought."

"Eyes, colour, shaven, unshaven? Anything that would help me pin him down?"

"On the way to the drop-off point, I heard one of the guys call him George."

"You sure it was 'George'?" Smethwick was getting excited.

"I'm sure. When we got to the warehouse in Bermondsey, I heard him talking to another man. I think I've seen him before. I think he's a policeman. I can't be sure."

"Sergeant, get the file from my case."

Smethwick took out a photograph of PC Graham. "Is this the man?"

O'Carroll looked at the photograph and said, "Yes, that's him."

"Sure?"

"Without a doubt."

"What's the address?"

O'Carroll was lost for a moment. "What address?"

"The warehouse?"

"Oh, I don't know. I can take you there."

O'Carroll was looking at a pile of photographs which Smethwick had retrieved from a folder. "Can I see that one, sir?"

He pointed to a fuzzy photograph. Smethwick handed it over.

O'Carroll studied it for a moment, then said, "That's one of the gang. He gave me five pounds. It's him."

Smethwick took the photo and turned it over. It was annotated as 'Liam Cartney'. He showed it to DS Routledge.

"So, what happened next?" Smethwick asked.

"I went home to Mary-Jane. On the way, I bought medicine for her. That man had a lot of money in his pocket. A big roll. I spent all of my money on Mary-Jane."

"The man with the money, what did he look like? The picture is blurred." Smethwick wanted to drain Brendan of every piece of information.

"He was slim. His hair was black with traces of grey at the sides. He spoke very quietly. I noticed his hands, soft, like he'd never done a hard day's work in his life."

"Name?" Smethwick insisted.

"I can't be sure."

Routledge leant across and said, "Sign this."

"What is it?" Brendan asked.

"It just says that you don't want a solicitor."

O'Carroll pulled a face. He signed it, nevertheless.

Smethwick and Routledge left the room. O'Carroll relaxed slightly, then put his head in his hands. He looked up as another man entered the room. He sat down and stared at Brendan.

He then nodded toward the police officer at the back of the room. He waited until they were alone.

"You have one option that will save you from the gallows." Arthur waited until the impact of what he'd said had sunk in.

"Excuse me, sir, who are you?"

"I'm an officer from the special branch. My name is irrelevant. I now have enough evidence to have you tried in secret for treason. The court will undoubtedly find you guilty. You'll hang. It's not a nice way to die."

"Sir, I've cooperated with the police. I don't know what else I can tell you. I'm an ex-soldier. I don't deserve to hang."

"The only reason I'm not having you pulled out in chains and exposed to the press is because you are an ex-soldier. I have read your military file. What went wrong? I know you are a murderer."

He held his hand up to stop O'Carroll from denying it.

"You strangled Hetherington. You also conspired to murder two police officers and now you are gunrunning and aiding an attack on this country with enemies foreign and domestic. Frankly, I would prefer to take you outside and shoot you myself. But my superiors say that I must not do that. So, you have a choice, die in agony hanging from a rope or help your country to thwart the upcoming attack?"

"Sir, I know of no attack. I don't know what these men intend to do with the weapons they...I stole."

"You could help if you were a member of their organisation. If they found out, they would undoubtedly shoot you. On the other hand, you could help arrest the lot and serve a short sentence, rather than hang. It's up to you. Think about it. I will be back."

Brendan O'Carroll sat in his cell pondering his fate. He had no convictions against helping the police. Apart from the murders and several petty thefts he had been involved in, he was basically a law-abiding citizen.

Hetherington's murder was an aberration. Theobald, Meeks, and Erskine's murders were done to protect Mary-Jane from the poor house. Everything he had ever done was to protect Mary-Jane.

He knew his life was over now. But Mary-Jane was his sole reason for accepting the role of a nark. He still hoped to find a way to ensure she was looked after, whatever fate his future held.

Fifteen

The Baron's Man

Smethwick insisted that O'Carroll should give a full and frank statement of all the murders he had been involved in. By the end of the day, Smethwick had the whole story of the Puddle Dock murders…with the one exception.

Brendan did not tell Smethwick about Mary-Jane's role in Theobald and Meeks' murders. The eye-opener was that they now knew the name of the anonymous body, Albert Erskine.

Smethwick and Routledge could relax now that they had O'Carroll. They had agreed to allow Brendan to work for the special branch, until the larger case was solved.

At no time had they agreed to overlook Brendan O'Carroll's crimes. It would be for a judge to decide if he should hang.

If their senior officers in the city police were unhappy that two of their best detectives were informally working for the Metropolitan police special branch, they did not let it be known.

Smethwick's job was to track down Maitland, Graham, Collins, and Liam Cartney's involvement in the dockyard robbery.

Jonas passed the details of the robbers to Arthur Middleton.

Brendan and Mary-Jane were transported to Clacton, Essex. This was supposed to give them an alibi for their disappearance from his job and home. Anyone asking about them were told they were on holiday. This would fit in with the five pounds Brendan had been given.

It was several weeks before the FoH took an interest in Brendan again. They were dismayed to find out that he had lost his job as a guard. His impromptu holiday was blamed. They needed him at that office. So, a welfare officer argued his case and the management allowed him back.

Brendan was grateful to be back at work. It was true that the special branch was paying him a small stipend for his services, but he had worked all his life; he needed to be busy.

Arthur was intrigued by the FoH's persistence in getting Brendan back into that job. They discreetly investigated the company. It was a Merchant Marine Insurance company with its headquarters in Cuxhaven, Germany.

Anti-German paranoia was increasing. Many newspapers were running articles which claimed that the Kaiser was intent on breaking up the empire or invading England.

Arthur Middleton's superiors were shocked by his detailed report into Merchant Marine. More resources were earmarked should the investigation turn up anything concrete.

Brendan found himself running errands for the company

secretary, a Prussian nobleman named Baron von Marburg. The baron appreciated Brendan's discipline.

After some time, the baron relaxed a little. He would talk to Brendan about the military differences between Germany and England. Brendan's opinions were ignored. The baron did not like to be contradicted.

Brendan soon learned to listen, in this way he realised that the Friends of Hibernia and the baron had many views that sat neatly together.

The special branch, with Brendan's help, was mapping out the baron's contacts.

Brendan was on a weekly trip to a bank in the West End. He had jumped on a bus and settled down. Arthur sat next to him. "What have we today?"

Brendan was expecting him. "A letter, not sure what it is. It's taped down and has a wax seal."

"Next week you will get off the bus at Piccadilly Circus. A colleague of mine will escort you to a nearby office. He's an expert. We need to get a look inside the next packet."

He then got up and left the bus. Brendan ignored him as he walked past the bus. He knew that sooner or later they would want to consider what he carried. He was getting nervous as he neared the bank. He delivered the letter without a hitch. He hoped the next one would be as easy.

The week went quietly, and Brendan was waiting for his usual trip. He was given a small parcel to take to the same bank. Everything went as usual until he alighted from the bus at Piccadilly.

He stood by the bus stop. He felt a tug on his arm. "You help me?"

The man had a heavy accent. He wore a trilby hat and a long raincoat. He was smart in a casual way. His clothes were good condition, but not the best. He had a beard and a small moustache. His glasses showed that his eyesight was not great.

"I have lost my way. Could you look at a map for me?"

"Of course, where do you want to go?" Brendan asked.

"Perhaps we could go to my office across the way."

The accent had changed, and the man had become more dominant. "Come, Mr O'Carroll, time is tight."

They both walked over to a small tobacconist. The man walked past the assistant behind the counter.

"Show me what you have."

Brendan removed the packet from his briefcase. The man looked it over. He had removed his spectacles. "Hmm, tight seams. The seal is one I have not seen before. Do you know what type of glue they use?"

"No, sir, I never see the packet before it's handed to me."

"Well, there's nothing I can do today. This one is the one that got away. Please deliver it."

Brendan was ushered out of the shop and walked toward his destination.

When he returned to the office, he was called into see the baron. He sat behind an impressive desk. The office manager stood by the desk and began to question Brendan.

"Why were you late? The bank said you were ten minutes late."

"I'm sorry, sir, I did not realise. It won't happen again."

"Where were you? Explain yourself!"

"I bought the baron a cigar. He told me he missed having a Cuban cigar. I knew of a shop that sold Cuban cigars and wanted to get him one. He's been so good to me, allowing me to return to my job."

The baron stood up "Where is it?"

Brendan unlocked his briefcase and removed one cigar wrapped in a cardboard case. He handed it over to the baron.

The baron examined it. He smiled. "It is expensive. How can you afford it?"

"I had a few shillings left over from my holiday. I wanted to say thank you, Herr Baron."

The baron smiled. "I thank you. Do not be late at the bank again."

"Yes, sir," said Brendan.

Heinrich Schiller told Arthur of his failed mission. They tried to think of ways of finding out what was in the packets. Schiller proposed X-rays. However, they would need the package for far too long.

Schiller had worked for the intelligence services for years. He was an expert in removing items and returning them without any suspicions being aroused. He set to work to find out where the seal came from. He would then create his own. Failing that, the SB would arrange for a burglary in the office and copy the seal.

***

Smethwick waited for the warehouse to be raided. Surveillance had shown that the building was protected by one guard. No other activity had been seen.

The Metropolitan police led the assault. Special branch had two of its officers with the local police. Nothing was found. The weapons had been moved. The guard was legitimately employed by the owners. Smethwick and Routledge arrived after the mass of officers had left.

After speaking to one of the SB officers, the two detectives did their own search of the premises. Any evidence would have to be handed over to the Met, but they hoped that something would be found.

Routledge upended a dustbin. Partially burnt newspapers were strewn across the floor. He noticed that the newspapers were mostly daily and evening papers. However, there was a large broadsheet which was burnt around the edges. Something about it was out of place. It was obviously an upmarket newspaper. He thought either *The Times* or *Telegraph*. He folded it and put it in his pocket. Nothing else was found.

Later that day, Routledge was sitting in Smethwick's office, reading the paper scrap. He scanned the paper numerous times. He was sure it was significant. Newspapers like *The Times* and *Telegraph* were not usually read by the working classes. Their favourite was *The Star*.

He was on the verge of giving up, when he saw a few words at the bottom of the page, near a section that was burnt away. The first line was in bold letters, 'King to vis…' The rest was burnt.

Routledge guessed that the line was 'King to visit' something or someone. He needed to read the full article to have a sense of its importance. He had no idea when the paper was printed. A trip to Fleet Street would give him the answers he needed.

The paper was identified as *The Times*. The story was that King Edward VII, with the Queen Alexandra, would sail Her

Majesty's yacht, *Victoria and Albert*, under Tower Bridge to celebrate its tenth anniversary since being opened.

The royals would then visit the bridge and watch its span being lifted. A dinner would be held on board the yacht for invited dignitaries later that evening.

HMY *Victoria and Albert* would then leave the Pool of London the next day and visit various cities around Great Britain.

Routledge showed the article to DI Smethwick and Arthur Middleton. Both agreed that this would be a perfect target for the enemies of England.

The celebrations were known by the authorities, but apart from the small piece in *The Times* newspaper, the visit's full details were only known by a select few. The tenth anniversary of the opening of Tower Bridge was the 30th of June 1904. They had less than six months before the event would take place.

Sixteen
The Assault

DI Smethwick was called to a meeting with the special branch, to discuss the possible attack against the king. The City of London Police, the Metropolitan police, special branch, and a member of the king's security team were assembled. Smethwick related what he knew about the activities of the Friends of Hibernia. Arthur Middleton expanded on the SB's current investigation into a possible German involvement.

The king's security man was sure that no one could infiltrate HMY. There was a general opinion that it would be inconceivable that the Kaiser would sanction an attack on the king. However, all the assembled officers were tasked with upgrading security and finding out what exactly the threat was.

***

Brendan O'Carroll was sure he was being followed to the bank each week. He spoke to no one, nor was approached by lost foreigners. Yet he had the feeling that someone was behind him.

On his next trip, he alighted from the bus and was only a quarter of a mile from the bank. He usually walked the last part. As he turned a corner, two ruffians jumped on him. He was battered to the floor and his briefcase was stolen. He was found by a police officer. Brendan was put in a Black Maria and taken to St Bart's hospital.

He was unconscious for two days; Mary-Jane visited him each day. On the third day, he came round. He was surprised to see the baron sitting next to his bed in a crowded, smelly public ward.

"You are feeling better?" the baron asked.

"A little better, sir. What happened?"

"You were attacked by ruffians. They took my letters. Did you know them?"

"No, sir, I don't remember much. I'm sorry about the letters."

The baron scanned Brendan's face and hands. The bruising was obvious and real. The pain that Brendan was feeling was clear to the baron.

"You will get better. Your job is safe, for the moment." He stood up and walked out of the ward.

Heinrich Schiller was busy examining the letters taken from Brendan. The first one he opened was a money order for two hundred pounds, made out to the Friends of Hibernia. The other letters were written in code. Each letter was copied by hand. All the letters were sealed again and placed in the briefcase. Schiller knew that the baron would be suspicious when the briefcase was returned to his company, but he was confident that no one would know that the contents had been opened and copied.

DI Smethwick was not informed that O'Carroll would be attacked and robbed. Two of Arthur's men had undertaken the assault. They hit Brendan several times, but each blow was aimed not to cause any permanent injury.

The codes were sent to military intelligence to decode.

A police officer returned the briefcase to the offices of Merchant Marine Insurance. The baron examined it and the contents for some time. Being naturally suspicious, he called in his own expert. He was firmly of the opinion that the letters had been tampered with. But was unsure whether they had been read.

Suspicion fell on Brendan again. He was taken off the bank run and returned to his original task of patrolling the premises.

When Smethwick found out about Brendan, he was determined to arrest him and charge him with the murders. As far as he was concerned, O'Carroll was now of no use to the German part of the conspiracy.

He would leave the rest of the case to the special branch. He had successfully solved the Puddle Dock murders. He was sure his superiors would agree with him and start committal proceedings. However, the special branch thought that O'Carroll could still be of use to them.

Smethwick was ordered to concentrate on the criminal case against Maitland and Graham. Special branch intended to use the city police to obscure their enquiries into the conspiracy and likely attack. They hoped that the FoH would not find out that the SB knew about their plans.

Brendan and Mary-Jane used the money they were receiving from the special branch wisely. They opened an account with the co-operative movement. Mary-Jane could now buy the necessary medicines for her condition.

Brendan knew that he was likely to either be arrested and hanged or murdered by the FoH when they found out about his duplicity. All he wanted was for Mary-Jane to be able to live comfortably after he was gone.

Arthur Middleton approached Brendan while he was walking home. A short conversation took place. Brendan nodded and went home.

Later that night, Brendan was waiting near the office in the Minories. A stranger approached him. They had a quiet conversation. Brendan handed over his keys.

At midnight, there was a knock on Brendan's front door. He opened it a little and peeked to see who it was. His keys were thrust into his hands. He closed the door quickly. The keys looked the same. None were missing. However, they had a slightly sticky residue on them. Brendan wondered what it was.

***

The baron was in early the next day. He looked at Brendan thoughtfully.

"Sergeant Major, you have your keys?"

"Of course, sir, they never leave my person."

"Show me."

Brendan unhooked them from his chain and handed them to the baron.

The baron took the keys and passed them to his manager, who walked away to the baron's office.

"Anything amiss, sir?" Brendan asked.

"We shall see. Yes, we shall see."

The manager returned after five minutes. The baron had never taken his eyes from Brendan's face.

"Well?"

The manager passed the keys back to Brendan.

"I can find nothing wrong with them, Herr Baron."

"You have a charmed life, Sergeant Major," The baron almost hissed. "But remember, lady luck is a fickle friend."

The baron turned away and walked back to his office, followed by the manager a few paces behind.

Brendan had remained at attention. He relaxed when the baron's office door was closed. The warning was clear to him. Whatever the men had done at the office had been found out. He wondered what would happen next.

Brendan's worst nightmare happened. Mary-Jane was attacked as she returned from picking up her medicines. Two men punched her to the ground and kicked her several times. Her purse and medicines were untouched. She was left unconscious; she was found by a passer-by.

Mary-Jane lay in a hospital bed, bandaged around the head. Her hands were purple with bruising. It was only when Brendan arrived at the hospital that the police and doctors could find out what had happened.

He sat holding her hand and praying that she would recover. As far as Brendan was concerned, the list of suspects was long. It was obviously a warning to him, but from who?

Brendan was asked to leave the ward soon after eight o'clock in the evening. The matron was adamant; family were only to visit during the designated visiting hours. She had allowed him some leeway, but nothing was to interfere with her routine.

Jonas Smethwick heard about the assault. He made some discreet enquiries. Detective inspectors usually ignore minor assaults. The gossip was rampant in Wood Street; why would a senior officer involve himself in an unremarkable street attack?

***

Since Smethwick had forced Maitland and Graham to flee, most of the other officers in Wood Street had kept their distance. They saw the DI as a threat to their careers. Already, several officers had been transferred. Those closest to Maitland and Graham had been investigated and suspended, pending further investigations.

Wood Street had been turned upside down by the continued investigations of Smethwick and Routledge. The activities of the Friends of Hibernia had effectively been neutralised in Wood Street.

Arthur Middleton was worried that the attack on Mary-Jane would weaken the hold special branch had on Brendan. He discreetly had Mary-Jane moved to her sister's home in Clacton. He needed Brendan to concentrate on getting all the necessary information about the forthcoming attack.

Jonas was equally perturbed. Why was the FoH so determined to keep Brendan involved?

Seventeen
The Kidnap

Franz Mizel sat opposite Saul, Liam, and Raul. They were meeting for the first time since getting the munitions for the attack on the crown.

They were meeting in Liam's flat in Covent Garden. The table was laden with meats, jam, tea, sugar, breads, and three bottles of wine. Liam and Franz had used a part of the conspiracy money for a last meal before they separated to take on their individual tasks.

As usual, Franz gave the welcome greeting. "Comrades, welcome. We meet to finalise the details of the beginning of the revolution. We have the men, arms, and transport to achieve all our aims. Tonight, we will put into action a plan that will shake England to its foundations."

Franz took Raul aside. "Any progress in getting an experienced gunner?"

"I had hoped to use an ex-artillery sergeant major. But he's under suspicion. The Friends believe he can be trusted but our sponsors are not so sure."

"Bring him here after Liam leaves next week. I will question him. If he is a spy, I will ask you to deal with him."

Raul nodded and said, "He has a wife…"

"No one should be left to thwart our plans. You understand?"

"Of course. Leave it to me."

Brendan was sitting in Liam's flat in Covent Garden. Raul Santiago stood behind him. They were waiting for Franz to return from running errands. Franz had effectively taken over the flat since Liam had gone to train for the attack.

Franz entered the flat and put down a bag of groceries. Brendan automatically stood to attention when he saw him.

"So, this is the sergeant major I have heard so many good things about. Please sit down. Our friends in the FoH have told me much of your work supporting the cause."

Brendan sat quietly listening to Franz. He was trying to pin down his accent. Brendan was acutely aware of the menacing figure standing behind him.

"Please, Raul, you are making the sergeant major nervous. Sit by me. We are all friends here, are we not?" Here he looked at Brendan.

"Of course, sir," Brendan answered.

Franz questioned Brendan about his service record. He did not ask about any murders. After an hour, Brendan was feeling drained. Franz had been thorough and had asked the same questions repeatedly but in a different format. Any mistakes or new information was minutely examined.

"Thank you, Sergeant Major. I need not keep you anymore. Please wait by the door for a moment."

"Well?" said Raul.

"I believe he is holding something back. However, it may be trivial. His knowledge would be helpful to us. We should watch him from now on. I can use him. You can remove him if he wanders from the plan."

"And his wife?"

"Perhaps she should be taken into protective custody by our friends. Just in case," Franz replied.

***

Alice, Mary-Jane's sister, was waiting outside Brendan's flat in the city. She was distraught when she saw him arrive home. After much sobbing and frequent, "I'm so sorry, I couldn't help her," from Alice, Brendan could piece together what had happened.

Late one night Alice and Mary-Jane were quietly sewing while Alice repeated the day's gossip. A knock on the door was heard and Alice walked to the window and saw a man in a police uniform. She opened the door and was manhandled to a seat and told to be quiet. Two other men entered and rushed at Mary-Jane. She was gagged and blindfolded and lifted off her feet by the men and taken out to a horse-drawn trap.

The policeman gagged and tied Alice to the seat. It was the next morning before she was found by the milkman.

Brendan had gone very quiet. He flexed his fists. He had tears in his eyes. This was the second attack on Mary-Jane, Brendan was determined that it would be the last.

He left Alice crying. He put on his overcoat and left the flat, heading to the office. No one was surprised to see him again. He was often called in to do extra hours or perform tasks for the baron.

However, what he did next left those that saw it frozen in shock. Brendan walked straight into the baron's office. Before any protest could be uttered, Brendan had pulled the baron out of his desk chair. He quickly grasped the baron around his neck and squeezed. The baron's eyes began to bulge. His tongue had swollen and was protruding from his mouth. He was trying to extricate himself from the grip on his throat. He could feel the pressure from the assailant's hands as it increased. He was slowly losing consciousness.

Throughout the attack, Brendan said nothing. His eyes had glazed over. All rational thought had left him. He wanted the baron dead. He was convinced that his men had kidnapped Mary-Jane.

The baron knew that it was over. His body went limp, and he passed out. Brendan continued the pressure. Despite the weight of the body, he held his victim in the same position. The screams of horror and fear suddenly seeped into his awareness.

He heard shouting in the room and running footfalls nearing him. At once he felt a blow on his head and then he crumpled to the floor.

The office manager and the baron's chauffeur had seen what was happening. Both had run to save their master. The chauffeur had struck Brendan across the back of his head with a cosh. It only needed one hit to disable him.

Eighteen

Missing

Arthur Middleton was worried. He contacted DI Jonas Smethwick and informed him of Brendan's disappearance. Jonas had DS Routledge make enquiries.

Brendan O'Carroll had not been seen since his wife had disappeared from the Clacton address. Enquiries at his work address proved fruitless. No one was speaking at the office. The manager had denied seeing him since he finished his shift, three weeks ago.

The baron was on holiday and was unavailable to interview.

DS Routledge had visited the staff from Merchant Marine at home. Everyone gave similar statements to each other. Archie was convinced that they had been coached. It was clear that they were frightened.

Without Brendan's weekly reports to Arthur Middleton, the special branch were now coming under pressure from military intelligence to find out how far the suspected attack had progressed.

Brendan's intelligence was often mundane, but when it was put together with other information, the special branch, military intelligence, and the Metropolitan police could identify many of the important suspects.

The various strands within law enforcement were now fighting to take over the lead in the investigation. The in-fighting was causing concern in the highest levels of government. All the parties were called together to work out a coherent strategy. Everyone was reminded that time was short.

DI Smethwick was given the job of finding Brendan. Arthur Middleton would then assess if he was still of use to thwart the conspiracy. Brendan would either continue to feed special branch with information or face arrest and be tried for the charges that were awaiting him.

Jonas knew that if he could find Mary-Jane, he would be able to manipulate Brendan to do anything he wanted. He was concerned, however, that he had no evidence that either of them were still alive.

His pessimism was further reinforced when DS Routledge gave him an update about Brendan.

"Sir, I was able to convince one of the secretaries at Merchant Marine to come clean about Brendan O'Carroll. It seems that O'Carroll attacked Baron von Marburg. He rushed into his office and strangled the baron. One of the baron's men hit Brendan with a cosh of some sort. She was unable to tell me whether the baron or Brendan were still alive. They were told not to talk about the incident, on pain of dismissal. They were later told that the baron had returned to Germany and Brendan had been dismissed."

"So, it's likely that Brendan is either captive or dead already. Do we know how the baron, or his body, got out of the country?"

"No, sir, I took the liberty of asking Mr Middleton to look into it."

"Well done, Archie. I think we must assume that Brendan is out of the picture now. We cannot do a great deal until we know whether he is alive and in what state of health. Perhaps we should use our time to find the other conspirators."

***

The baron had arrived home after spending three weeks in a clinic on the shores of the North Sea. He was still shaky and heavily bruised around his neck. He found it difficult to speak. His arrogance had suffered a setback, but he was determined to make the culprit pay with is life.

His nurse gave him a soothing warm drink. He was looking out toward the surf. He motioned for her to leave. The office manager stood at attention ready to answer the baron's questions.

"Is he still alive?" he said very quietly.

"Yes, Herr Baron."

"Where is he?"

"In the cellar, Herr Baron."

"Have they found out why he attacked me?"

"Yes, Herr Baron, it appears that he suspected you of

kidnapping his wife. She disappeared, taken by two men. She has not been seen since."

The baron was quiet for a while.

"Did we?"

"No, Herr Baron, my investigations have named the Friends of Hibernia as the culprits. It seems that they wanted leverage over him. He has been spying on your movements, who you meet and passing the information to Franz Mizel."

The baron sipped his drink. "Mizel, I should have known. Did our agent know of this?"

"It appears that Signor Santiago arranged the kidnap. But he denies knowing that Franz Mizel was using O'Carroll to spy on you."

"Do you believe him?"

"I have never trusted him but, on this occasion, I do believe him, Herr Baron."

"On Friday I will interview O'Carroll. Ask the Hauptmann to soften him up a little. Under no circumstance must he be killed. I have other plans for him."

The baron waved his hand to dismiss the manager. He sat looking out at the roaring North Sea.

"After the plan has succeeded, they will pay," he said aloud.

He rang a bell for a servant to help him to his escritoire. The servant was dismissed. He began to write a letter. It was passed to his aide, who coded it, and took it to the wireless operator stationed in the loft.

***

Liam Cartney had spent the last few months training to use firearms. His conscience was clear. News from Ireland had been bad. Several of his fellow revolutionaries had been arrested. Two had been hanged.

Reports from sympathisers in the UK had spoken of increased police activity. They had many questions about what was happening in anarchist circles. They obviously knew something was happening but did not have enough evidence to act.

Liam knew that he was under surveillance. He had seen the same faces in various locations across London. He had taken buses when he was aware of the men following him. It took him twice as much time to meet other members of the conspiracy.

On occasions, he had missed appointments rather than put the others at risk. He received an urgent request from a sympathiser. Franz needed to talk to him.

He set off for the rendezvous point and was arrested by Inspector Maurice Holcombe.

"Liam Cartney, I am arresting you for gunrunning and sedition, you do not have to say anything…" After the caution, Holcombe said to Liam, "At last, I've got you, you Fenian bastard. You'll hang. And I'll be there to witness it."

Liam knew his time had come. But he would not go quietly.

"I am terribly sorry, Officer, you have the wrong man. My name is Terrence Nightingale. I am a trainee solicitor in London."

He smiled broadly at Holcombe.

"Yes, and my auntie smokes a pipe. You're Liam Cartney, and I'll prove it."

"Officer, may I show you my identification? It's in my inside pocket."

The officers holding his arms looked at Holcombe, he nodded. One arm was freed. Liam drew out a wallet and passed it to Holcombe.

Inside was documentation that identified Liam as Terrence Nightingale. A document showed that he was a trainee solicitor with the Friends of Hibernia, a charitable organisation.

Holcombe was confused but determined to take him in. He was sure he had Cartney.

Within half an hour, the FoH had heard about Liam's arrest. A solicitor was dispatched to Holloway police station.

Liam sat in an interrogation room. Holcombe and a Met officer sat opposite him, waiting for the solicitor. Mr Ralph Fitzsimmons entered the room, he acknowledged the officers and then said, "Well, Terrence, what have you been up to?"

"A misunderstanding, sir. This officer believes I am a wanted man." He smiled broadly.

Holcombe said, "Your name is?"

"Sorry, Fitzsimmons, I am Mr Nightingale's tutor, and now his solicitor. Could you tell me why you have arrested my client?"

"I believe this person to be Liam Cartney. He is wanted here and in Ireland. The warrant charges him with gunrunning and sedition."

"I see. And when was he supposed to have committed these offences?"

Holcombe looked at his paperwork, then said, "1897 to 1899. Various dates inclusive."

"May I?" Fitzsimmons asked.

Holcombe passed over the charge sheet.

"I see. That would mean that my client was gunrunning while being tutored by me. Mr Nightingale was signed by me in November 1897. Here are his papers."

Holcombe read the papers and passed them to the Met officer. He read them and passed them back to the solicitor. He said nothing.

"On a personal note, Inspector, I have known Terrence since he was a youngster in Dublin. I know his family. I also note that you are wearing an orange order pin on your lapel. Could this be a case of wishful thinking on your part? I believe you also called my client a 'Fenian bastard'. That is not the language one expects of a senior officer. You may be able to get away with that behaviour in the special branch, but we expect police officers to be truthful and show a modicum of decency."

"I resent that. How dare you…bloody…" The Met officer leant across and gripped Holcombe's arm. It was enough to stop him mid-sentence.

"There's obviously been a mistake. Mr Nightingale is free to go. I apologise for keeping you."

"Thank you, Officer. May I have your name for my report?"

"Of course, Detective Inspector Williams."

Liam and Fitzsimmons rose from the table and walked out of the room. A few words were passed between Fitzsimmons and the desk sergeant. Liam and the solicitor hailed a cab and drove off much relieved.

Nineteen
Execution

For the past five weeks, Brendan had been incarcerated in the baron's cellar. Every day since he was taken from the baron's office, he had been assaulted. The first weeks were the worst. His inquisitors wanted information.

"Why did you attack the baron?" The questioner was quietly spoken. He had a heavy accent.

"Sir, the baron had my wife, Mary-Jane, kidnapped. He also had her attacked."

"Why would he do that?"

"Trying to control me."

"I do not understand. Why would he want to control you? You are like a bug. He could squash you whenever he likes. Who paid you to attack the baron?"

"No one, I swear on Mary-Jane's life."

"Mary-Jane is tot – Er, dead. She died under interrogation. She was braver than you, she did not say a word."

Brendan began to sob quietly.

"Why are you working for Franz Mizel? We know you are spying for him. You must answer me, or you will end up next to Mary-Jane in the pig food."

The interrogator nodded to his colleagues who rained blows over Brendan's body. They followed up the punches with freezing cold water from the North Sea.

He told them everything he knew.

The questions went on and on. The questioners were particularly interested in what part Franz Mizel had played. They did not like it when he told them he had never met him. They described him. He had to admit meeting him once. They hit him again.

Over the weeks, the questions had dried up, but the assaults had continued. They then introduced psychological torture. Brendon was a strong man, but all the talk of Mary-Jane was getting to him. He was beginning to lose heart.

"You know, your wife was stronger than you, even when we hit her, she refused to talk. Not like you, coward."

The image of Mary-Jane being tortured and knowing that she could not talk nearly drove him mad. When the baron finally entered the cellar, he saw a broken man. No longer the straight-backed sergeant major, but a wreck of a man. Brendan had multiple bruises over his face and chest. The fingers on his left hand had been broken. The baron stared at Brendan. He smiled.

"So, Sergeant Major, you have survived this part of your interrogation. You will not survive the rest."

Brendan looked at the baron. "It seems you have too, Herr Baron."

At that moment, the leader of the interrogators slapped Brendon hard across the face.

"You will be respectful to the Herr Baron."

The baron smiled again.

"I have decided to have you shot. You will face the firing squad tomorrow at dawn. I do this out of respect for your service to your country."

"Thank you, Herr Baron. Please, what has happened to my Mary-Jane? Please let her live."

"I fear you have been misinformed. I, nor my men, did not abduct your wife. It's true I know who did, and they will pay. I cannot guarantee her safety yet, for I do not know if she is alive or not."

"But they said…"

"In war, one must use all weapons, to acquire the truth."

Brendan began to cry. Quiet sobs at first and then heartrending cries. His body shook uncontrollably. The baron nodded to his men. They left the cellar.

"I suggest you make peace with your God; at dawn you die a soldier's death. How I envy you."

***

Detective Inspector Williams drafted a report about Holcombe's behaviour. It landed on the desk of the special branch chief inspector. He read the report and knew the significance straight away. He passed it on to Arthur Middleton to deal with.

Arthur was in a quandary. He was under instructions not to allow the evidence of the conspiracy to get out. Should the FoH get to hear of his interest in Liam Cartney, there was a possibility that they would know that the authorities were aware of their plans.

Inspector Holcombe had not shown himself to be very bright. He was likely to blunder into his investigation and cause problems. Arthur drafted another report to the chief suggesting that Holcombe be moved away from HQ to ensure he did not interfere with the investigation. Holcombe found himself checking passenger details in Heysham Docks the very next week.

DI Smethwick and Arthur Middleton met at the pie shop in Shoreditch. It was not a happy meeting. Without Brendan's intelligence, the case was stagnating.

They both assumed that Brendan and Mary-Jane were dead. Who had done it was still a mystery. Arthur related the information about Liam Cartney.

"We had him. Can you believe it? He was locked up. All Holcombe had to do was tell his boss. He would have had a commendation and I could have interrogated Cartney. We could have cracked the case open."

"Where's Holcombe now?" Jonas asked.

"Stuck in the country. Checking for illegal pig smuggling, for all I care."

"Any information on the O'Carrolls?" Arthur asked.

"Not a thing, how about on your side?"

"Not really." He paused.

"Go on. What do you know?"

"Not know, suspect," Jonas replied.

"My sources suggest that Brendan and the baron were taken to a German registered vessel the day after the attack.

Both were stretchered onto the vessel."

"Is your source dependable?"

"He has been good in the past, but he has a problem with the bottle. I have had him watch Brendan, quietly, since we recruited him. The problem is, when he runs out of grog, he makes things up. If it is true that they have gone to Germany, then we have reached a dead end."

Jonas played with his pie. Finally, he put down his fork.

"You know what that could mean?" Arthur interrupted, "The attack is imminent."

"Yes, I cannot bear to think about the consequences of such an attack."

Guido brought the bill and looked at the uneaten pies. He saw the worried look on the two patrons and decided against saying anything.

As they waited for a cab, Arthur said, "Incidentally, I found out yesterday that the solicitor who represented Liam Cartney left for the USA. It seems he will be working for the FoH in Boston. And, of course, Cartney has disappeared again."

"Rats leaving a sinking ship," said Jonas.

"Looks that way," Arthur replied.

Twenty
Mary-Jane

U do read the message again. It had taken him nearly an hour to decrypt it. The meaning was clear. He set it on fire. The encryption book, radio and blank message slips were put back into the chimney.

Udo reread the message. It was a death warrant for all the main participants in the conspiracy. Franz Mizel headed the list, then Saul, Liam, O'Carroll and a new name, Raul Santiago. The FoH participants had been given a crucial yet highly dangerous task. The baron was not expecting any of them to survive. If anyone did, Udo would deal with them.

The plan details had shifted. The anarchists were to be isolated. More German recruits would be engaged to take their position. It would be a wholly German affair, even if the FoH thought differently.

Udo was not concerned. He knew that he was unlikely to survive. He had a plan, just in case, but it was risky.

Raul Santiago was waiting for his new contact in Hyde Park after the baron's departure. A small man dressed in quite shabby clothes sat next to him. The man looked like a clerk in an office. He began to feed the pigeons with bread.

Raul watched him with contempt.

"This seat is taken, here." Raul held out a penny, "Take this and go."

The man smiled and continued to feed the birds.

"Did you hear me? Go away, I'm meeting someone. Move or I will hurt you." He pulled a knife out.

"Ah, Herr Santiago? You are meeting me. Please put the weapon away. I have my own." He moved his coat a little. A pistol could be seen in his belt.

"The Herr Baron would like an update on the..." Here he paused and said, "Affair."

"Cartney was arrested, but we got him away. He is now secreted with the boat. The men are trained, and the weapons are also ready. Our only problem is the loss of Brendan O'Carroll. He was to be our gunner."

"The baron has this man. You will have him back soon. The baron is concerned that some of your team may be veering from the designated target. Do you know anything of this matter?"

"I'm not sure what you mean?"

"What of the man's wife? She was taken, was she not?"

"I heard that the FoH had her. Simply to ensure O'Carroll's cooperation."

"And you did not help them? You are not forgetting your oath, are you?"

"Of course not. I'm committed to the baron, as always."

"Good, the baron wants the woman back. You must retrieve her. The baron will be back next week. You have five days to get her. Failure is not an option. Why not use the boat expert…what is his name?"

"Udo, his name is Udo Lebensberger."

"Excellent, I will inform the baron of your continued loyalty." The shabby man stood up and ambled away.

Raul sat for some time on the bench. It was clear that the baron had misgivings about him. Perhaps getting the woman was a test. Fail and he would disappear.

***

Two of the baron's men came for Brendan. They pinioned his arms behind his back and marched him out of the cellar. As his eyes adjusted to the early morning sun, he saw a stake in front of a wall.

They indicated that he should walk toward it. He walked slowly, savouring the sun on his face. A third man stood waiting for him.

Brendan was spun around and pushed against the stake. Two straps held him fast. The man put a blindfold over his eyes. He heard the click of the rifles being cocked.

He said a silent prayer. His last words were, "I love you, Mary-Jane."

There was a crash as three rifles were fired. Brendan fell forward. The ropes held him in place. He felt no pain. He slowly lifted his head. He heard footsteps coming toward him, he expected to feel a pistol at his temple, the coup de grâce.

The baron lifted the blindfold from Brendan's eyes.

"I apologise, Sergeant Major, my men loaded the wrong ammunition. I will deal with them later. Unfortunately, I have a meeting soon. So therefore, we will have to postpone your execution. Take him back to the cellar."

Over the next week, he was dragged out to the stand in front of the firing post. He knew that one morning they would shoot him. In times of despair, he would beg the Lord to end his pain.

The baron knew exactly what signs to look for. Brendan was a strong man. But he had his Achilles' heel, Mary-Jane.

The baron had been searching for Mary-Jane since her kidnap. Information had come from his agents in England that Raul Santiago had rescued her from her captors.

She was now on her way to Germany.

Mary-Jane lay on a bed in a storage room on a German trawler, she was seasick. It was the first time she had been on a real boat. At first her captors had tied her hands and feet. But it became clear that she was no sailor. She now had the freedom to roam the small space. However, as soon as she stood up, she was sick. Laying down was the only way to deal with the boat's motion.

The guards took turns to laugh at her. They would hold food in front of her. The smell was enough to make her sick again. She was left alone for most of the voyage. One of the sailor's took an unhealthy interest in Mary-Jane. He would stroke her hair and call her his 'kleine Puppe' (Little doll).

Mary-Jane was resting from another bout of dry heaving. when she heard the door being opened. A little light spread out into the space. The sailor who had taken an interest in her was creeping in. Mary-Jane did not move. As he neared where she was, he was whispering in German. She felt his hand on her knee. She had feared that something like this may happen.

As the sailor moved his hands further up her body she lay absolutely still. He must have thought she was an easy target; he knew she could not scream. At the same time Mary-Jane swung the chamber pot which she had secreted next to her. The heavy porcelain pot crashed into his head. He rolled over unconscious. The noise was heard, and other sailors rushed in. The sailor was dragged out. The captain was berating the sailor. A scream was heard and then a loud splash. The attacker was never seen again.

Brendan had spent all of the night thinking about Mary-Jane. He had no idea where she was. He heard the guards opening the cellar door. He prayed that this would be the day they conducted the execution. He did not struggle as he walked ahead of them.

In the garden he waited until the baron had inspected the firing squad's weapons. Satisfied, Brendan was pushed toward the stake.

They tied him. He refused the blindfold. He was at the end of his tether. He wanted this to be the end. Unusually, the guard gagged him. Brendan struggled but it was done.

As he waited for the guards to line up, he noticed the baron smirking. When the firing squad was ready, the baron nodded. Brendan waited for the bullets to tear into him. Instead, the guards lowered their rifles.

There was a commotion as one of the guards dragged a

female into the garden. Brendan could not believe his eyes. Mary-Jane was standing not more than fifteen feet from him.

As soon as Mary-Jane saw him, she began to struggle and fight her captors. It took two of them to subdue her.

The baron was handed a sword. He examined it and then lifted it into the air. The guards resumed the shooting position.

Brendan never took his gaze off Mary-Jane. She began to struggle again. The baron dropped the sword in a slashing motion. The guards fired their weapons.

Mary-Jane saw the bullets go into the wall. Little puffs of dirt flew up. At that moment, she was sure that Brendan had been shot.

From deep in her being, a scream emanated from her mouth. In that moment, her years of frustration and despair merged into a terrifying burst of energy.

The scream was heard by all in that garden and the nearby mansion. The baron dropped the sword and the firing squad turned in her direction startled.

Brendan felt the bullets pass him. He had closed his eyes the moment he heard the rifles discharge. The scream brought him back to his senses and he looked in her direction.

He saw her on the ground, surrounded by the baron's men. He tried to break the bonds that held him but remained securely tied. He was sobbing and shouting out her name from beneath his gag.

Mary-Jane was lifted and taken into the house. The baron looked at Brendan with contempt. He picked up his sword again and walked toward him. He hit him in the face with the hilt of the sword. The blow rendered him unconscious.

***

DI Jonas Smethwick, DS Archie Routledge and Arthur Middleton sat in the pie house quietly discussing the conspiracy case. They had come to a dead end.

They had no leads. Brendan and Mary-Jane had disappeared. Liam Cartney had gone underground, and the original suspects, PC Maitland and PC Graham, had also disappeared. The baron was assumed to be in Germany. It was not known if he was returning to England.

"I have no appetite today," said Jonas. He pushed away his plate and sipped his wine.

"Sir?" said DS Routledge. "I was looking into Franz Mizel's background. O'Carroll said in his last report, before disappearing, that he thought Mizel was one of the leaders of the conspiracy. This got me to thinking, so I dug up all that the authorities know about him."

"Go on," said Jonas.

"Well, it seems that Mizel is well known in anarchist circles in this country. However, one would have expected him to be known on the continent too. But no, Franz Mizel is not known to the authorities. Doesn't that seem a little strange?"

"It is not unusual for anarchists to change their names when fleeing the authorities," Arthur Middleton mused.

"All of our other leads have come to nothing. But we have one source that we haven't investigated."

"Sergeant, do get to the point," Jonas said sharply.

"The only link we have at present is his bookshop in Holborn. I know that special branch were watching the shop. But their interest lay in Liam Cartney. They have since taken the surveillance away."

"Of course, how remiss of me. I should have investigated the link between Mizel and Cartney. Truthfully, until O'Carroll mentioned Mizel we thought of him as an unimportant fellow. But all our resources were bent on finding Cartney and then O'Carroll. Well done, Sergeant." Middleton smiled.

Jonas's mood brightened a little. "So, we concentrate on finding Mizel."

"If I may, sir?" Routledge interjected, "In my research, I noted that the rent is still being paid each month. It is always paid in cash, at a solicitor's office off the Gray's Inn Road. It is due next week, on Monday."

"You are not suggesting that Mizel will turn up, are you?"

"It is a possibility. If he does, we can either arrest him or trail him back to where he is living."

"A longshot, Sergeant. But it is the only lead at present," Jonas said.

The payment office was situated in a nondescript building next to a public house. Clients were recommended to go to the top floor. The stairs were tightly wound. A bare gas lamp was situated on each landing. The office was small and cramped. A lady sat at a desk typing. The senior clerk sat by the only window. His desk was neat but full of ledgers stacked high. A junior clerk sat at a desk placed before the entrance.

A knock was heard at the door. It opened at once. When the clerks saw who it was, they both stood up.

"Good afternoon, sir, I hope you are well?" the senior man said.

"Yes, thank you. I am fine." English was clearly not his first language. "The rent, please."

"Of course, sir. Edward?" The junior jumped at his name.

"The documents are ready for you, sir."

The gentleman smiled at the youth. "Thank you."

He examined the papers and then felt for his wallet in his inside pocket.

At the same moment, the door was thrown open and two uniformed police officers entered and immediately took the gentleman's arms.

Jonas Smethwick entered the room and stood in from of the startled man. "I am Detective Inspector Smethwick; I am arresting you for conspiracy to commit treason and other crimes. I require you to go with me to Paddington Green police station for questioning."

The officers removed the man. Jonas spoke to the others in the room. "Who is in charge?"

The senior clerk moved forward. "My name is Samuel Givens, I am the chief clerk."

"My sergeant will question you about the man taken away. Also, you must not speak to anyone about this incident."

Jonas walked down the stairs. He saw the suspect being put in a Black Maria. Arthur Middleton came up to him. "Is it Mizel?"

"I am almost certain." Jonas was smiling broadly.

They both watched as the vehicle disappeared into the traffic.

Twenty-One
Captured?

B rendan O'Carroll was once again in the cellar. He was nursing a small wound to his arm. It had been bandaged but was still weeping blood.

The baron's intention was to have the firing squad fire on each side of Brendan. It was to be his last fake execution. However, the unexpected scream from Mary-Jane had unnerved one of the squad. He had shot Brendan in the arm.

"So, Sergeant Major, it seems you are to live after all."

The baron had entered the cellar quietly.

"Where's Mary-Jane? I want to see her."

"You will see her if and when, I decide. Your wife will be my guest for the foreseeable future. You should concentrate on the upcoming task."

"I want your guarantee that Mary-Jane will not be hurt."

"You cannot demand guarantees from me. I will have both of you shot if you do not comply."

"I will do anything you want. Just don't hurt her. I'm begging you."

"You will be returned to England later today. Your task is to rejoin the work you were recruited to do. Report to me about Franz Mizel, his plans, actions, who he contacts and any digression from the plans. Do you understand?"

"What about Mary-Jane?"

"Mein Gott, Mary-Jane again. Do as you are told, and you and your wife will be together again."

"Alive?" Brendan demanded.

"Who knows? In war, anything can happen. Now, do not mention her again."

Brendan was allowed to see Mary-Jane before being taken to a boat to take him to England. He managed to give her a quick kiss before being parted again.

***

The middle-aged gentleman from the rent office sat quietly in the cell. Since his arrest, he had said nothing. Jonas and Arthur were looking at him through a wire grill in the door of the interrogation room.

"I suspect he is going to be difficult to break. He appears totally calm. No questions. No indignation at being arrested," Arthur remarked.

"I fear you may be right," replied Jonas.

"Has he asked for a solicitor?" Arthur enquired.

"No. We will see. Would you like to start, or shall I?"

"I think you should start. I can come in with the treason consequences, when necessary," Arthur said.

Jonas introduced himself and Arthur. A caution was given. The suspect said nothing and smiled.

"Your name is Franz Mizel, you are wanted for conspiracy to commit an act of treason."

The man said nothing.

"It would be in your best interests to come clean. We know about the plan. You will not get away with it." Jonas stared at the man. "My colleague will be happy to explain the consequences of your actions if you like?"

Still nothing was said.

Arthur then started to talk. "The penalty for treason is to hang by the neck until you are dead. I have seen it many times. It is not pleasant. If you are lucky, the neck is broken at once. On the other hand, if the knot is not placed properly, the subject is strangled slowly. They gasp for air, wriggle like a fish on the line. The tongue protrudes and can be bitten off in the throes of death. I have known it to last for a long time."

Jonas interrupted, "In the past, the hangman would pull on the feet of the victim. To hasten death. That is not allowed anymore. It is quite gruesome and, I believe, painful."

The man reached into his pocket and retrieved a handkerchief. He mopped his brow and wiped his hands.

Jonas and Arthur glanced at one another.

"Of course, that need not happen to you. You merely have to tell us all you know about the plan, the names of the others and where and when it will take place. What do you say?" Arthur sat back and waited for the answer.

The suspect coughed and said, "I would like to talk to my solicitor, please."

The interview was stopped while the solicitor was contacted.

"We have him," Arthur said excitedly.

"I am not sure. Something is wrong. I can feel it." Jonas shook his head.

***

Brendan had been locked in a cabin on a German fishing boat heading for somewhere in England. He had no idea how long he had been incarcerated.

At last, he heard the engines slowing. Within twenty minutes the boat had stopped. He heard shouts and orders as the crew tied the vessel to the dock. It was another day before he was released.

When finally released, Brendan saw that he was on the Thames near the estuary. The boat was tied to a dock outside a large warehouse. A slip appeared from the warehouse. Inside he saw a boat. He recognised its class as a Thames barge. There were many plying their trade up and down the river.

A man approached him. "Good morning, Sergeant Major. Nice to see you."

Brendan's face was discoloured, swollen, and bruised. He recognised the man. It was PC Maitland. He was now dressed in overalls and was wiping his hands with a rag.

"PC Maitland, nice to see you too."

"I am no longer a policeman. You can call me 'Sir'. You will do as you're told. You are free to go anywhere within the confines of the wire perimeter. Just in case you get itchy feet, Conrad," here he motioned to a very large man, standing behind Brendan, "will accompany you. Consider him your shadow."

Brendan looked at Conrad and nodded. Conrad was also a military man; his bearing was obvious to Brendan.

"Now, Sergeant Major, to work. We have several men waiting to learn the finer points of artillery from you. This way."

***

In Paddington Green police station, Arthur and Jonas waited while the solicitor met with his client. The officers entered the interrogation room.

"Officers, my client is willing to speak to you. Please ask your questions."

Jonas started first, "For the record, please state your name and occupation?"

"My name is Gerhart Eberhart. I am an accountant. I presently live in London. I am originally from Dresden."

Arthur almost shouted, "No you are not. You are Franz Mizel."

"No. I am Gerhart Eberhart. I can prove it."

"No doubt false documents, just like the lies you are telling us," Arthur replied.

The solicitor interrupted. "I can assure that he is who he says he is."

"Why were you paying the rent for Franz Mizel's bookshop?" Jonas asked.

"In fact, the bookshop is mine. I own it. Franz is my cousin. I allow him to live there. He makes a few pounds, which I allow him to keep. It is better to have it occupied rather than empty."

"When was the last time you spoke to him?"

"I have not spoken to or seen Franz for eighteen months, Inspector. I do not hold the same views as Franz. We argue. However, he is my blood relative. When he arrived in England, he came to see me. He wanted money. I had none at the time. So, I allowed him to take a room at the bookshop. It was he who made the shop practical. He could have stayed there and made a living, but he started to meet his old anarchist friends. I heard that the police were taking an interest in him. I decided not to associate with him."

"Did you inform the authorities that this man was dealing with anarchists?" Arthur asked.

"I did not."

"I am curious as to why you did not identify yourself when we arrested you?" Jonas asked.

"Sir, over the years I have been harassed, brutalised, and locked up, simply for being Franz Mizel's cousin. I lost my job as a professor of mathematics at Dresden University. I now must earn a living as an accountant. It is not the same. I avoid all associations with the authorities. I wish to live peacefully unhindered by questions about my family."

"If you do not cooperate with us, I can easily have you deported as an enemy alien," Arthur said.

"No threats, please, gentlemen," the solicitor interjected. "My client wants no trouble. He is more than willing to help in any way he can."

Jonas said, "That is all we want. What can you tell us of Franz's whereabouts?"

"I have none. However, the man you know as Franz Mizel, is named Franz Switzer. He changes his name often, to avoid the authorities. I believe he uses 'Lietsmann' at present."

"Inspector, my client has cooperated. Will you allow us to go?"

"Not until I have checked out his identity." Jonas did not want to make the same mistake as Holcombe and let a suspect get away.

Gerhart Eberhart was released two hours later. Arthur Middleton had Eberhart followed. Just in case he was not a clean as believed.

Jonas and Arthur watched as Eberhart and his solicitor left the police station. Jonas remarked to Arthur, "I wonder how he knew that Franz had changed his name?"

"Yes. If I was a suspicious type, I would also wonder," Arthur replied.

"I take it that you are having him tailed?"

"Of course," Arthur replied.

Twenty-Two
The Boatyard

Brendan O'Carroll's day in the boatyard was very stressful. The strain of being watched all day and night was wearing on him. The workforce all seemed to be German. They did not speak to anyone. Brendan recognised the way they operated. He had no doubt that they were military.

The few men from the Friends of Hibernia kept away from the Germans and him. He recognised one or two people. Maitland and Graham were there organising the Irish volunteers.

Franz nodded in recognition when they passed each other. Brendan noted that Franz and the one that had been at the weapons robbery, identified by Jonas as Liam Cartney, kept to themselves. It was the last time he saw either of them at the boat shed.

The yard was a hive of activity. The workmen worked in shifts. All the people in the yard were working to a strict timetable. Mistakes were punished heavily.

Brendan noticed that a partition was being erected on the front of the barge. Carpenters had built a platform. It was sturdy and securely fixed to the barge's timbers.

The headman motioned to Brendan. He spoke no English, but Brendan's shadow translated. He pulled back a tarpaulin from a small cannon. Other men ran forward and attached it to a winch and lifted on to the platform.

Brendan smiled. He recognised the cannon from his service in India. It was an Armstrong RM L 7-pr, 200 pounds, Mark 1. He was well acquainted with this piece of ordnance. He had used it as a young gunner.

Through his shadow, the headman asked if Brendan knew how to use it.

"Of course, I cut my teeth on the Armstrong. This is a powerful weapon. You'll need to secure it properly."

The headman laughed. "Ja, Ja."

Later that night, Brendan realised that with such a powerful cannon, the target was in big trouble. He had been told that he was to train several men to fire the cannon, in case of casualties. It suddenly hit him that the FoH and the baron were intent on waging a war; but against whom?

Brendan awoke in the middle of the night. The work had not stopped. He could not sleep. A question was turning over in his mind. If the workers were soldiers, it was likely that some were gunners. There was no reason to have him there.

The only reason he could come up with, was that he was to be a sacrificial lamb. They needed someone to blame. Why not a disaffected ex-soldier?

He walked around the yard. The guards kept him under

surveillance. They were all armed. He could see the weapons clearly. No guard strayed a foot away from a rifle, pistol, or other weapon. No one outside the yard had any idea of the firepower hidden within its surroundings.

Brendan made a mental note of the number of guards, where any loopholes were or whether he could get away from the compound. It was obvious that he was not dealing with amateurs.

He walked over to a trestle table, where there were snacks and tea for the workers. He poured a cup out and drank a little.

Back in his cot, he thought about everything that had happened since he had been brought to the yard. This was not a small affair. He participated in something well planned and audacious; something that he was unlikely to escape unharmed.

Despite being considered a weak link by the Germans in charge of the barge refit, Brendan was generally liked by the other workers. His strength was called upon to help manhandle a heavy joist or piece of equipment.

By the time that the refit was finished, the barge had a number of features not seen on the others. A large tarpaulin was neatly hiding the Armstrong cannon. The gunwales were eighteen inches higher around the barge. They were made of iron plate. Each yard or so, a hole was cut out. It was large enough to shoot through and offer some protection for the shooter to remain relatively safe.

At the rear of the barge, behind the wheel, another platform had been erected. On it stood a machine gun. It was capable of firing two hundred and fifty .303 rounds a minute.

The engineers had made it possible to slide on rails from one side to the other. It was high enough to fire over those in the gunwale. A team of four would ensure that its devastating power was used to make certain that the barge would get to its target unhindered.

The barge was painted in patriotic colours. The masts were adorned with gaily coloured pennants. Everything about it was aimed at allowing it to fit into the patriotic flotilla that was sure to assemble on the day of the attack.

Its firepower, it was hoped, would wipe out the target with little trouble. Below decks it had been fitted with explosives if the attack failed.

They were hidden from everyone except Udo Lebensberger, who would captain the vessel, and the baron with his second-in-command, the Hauptmann.

The Hauptmann inspected the vessel. He looked at the sails. They were rolled up on the various spars and masts. He called Udo.

"What if there is no wind? How do we get to our target?"

Udo thought for a moment. "We need an engine."

"How long to fit one?"

"Perhaps a week. That is, when I can find one," Udo replied.

"As quickly as possible, the baron will not be pleased by this omission."

Udo went off with the foreman to find an engine big enough to power the barge.

Brendan saw the Hauptmann and four men walking quickly toward him.

"Time to move, Sergeant Major. We have decided that your ability is no longer needed. Go with these men. Do not make any trouble."

Brendan was bundled into the back of a truck with two armed guards.

Twenty-Three

Captivity

After Franz and Liam had visited the boatyard, the two men walked towards a railway station near Dagenham. They were worried by what they had seen. The work was going well, but something was gnawing at Liam.

"Franz, how much money is left from the original thousand pounds?"

"About two hundred," he replied.

"So how can we afford to buy that barge and all the munitions? The arms we stole could not possibly be enough for such a large vessel?"

"I know. There is something amiss. I just cannot decide what."

"When you were speaking to the foreman, I had a look in a corner. I saw a cannon and a machine gun hidden. I know they were not part of the Woolwich haul," Liam said.

"This is not our plan. A small boat, several men moving

fast, and the target is taken. Light arms, swift action. This is more like a military assault."

They both looked at each other.

Liam said, "Did you notice that quite a few of the working men were speaking German?"

"I know. I asked one of them what union chapter they were with. He had no idea what I was talking about; just smiled. He was not a comrade, I think," Franz said.

"If they are not comrades, they could be a security risk. Except, we saw the FoH men, the policemen and the sergeant major."

"I know. I am worried by the chance that the Germans have infiltrated our plan. They are not sympathetic to the cause. Do we know for definite that the money we received was from anarchist sympathisers on the continent?" Franz replied.

"Raul would know. He arranged it. He has met the financiers."

"I have seen this before. Plans betrayed for money or by agent-provocateurs. The last time it was German military intelligence. My wife and child died."

Franz walked on. Liam had stopped for a moment. He looked behind him. He thought he saw someone hide quickly. He caught up to Franz.

"Do you suspect Raul?"

"No. I have questions though."

"Raul always seems to have money; money to spend, I mean."

"This is what happens. We begin to suspect a comrade. He resents us and we lose a good man. I want to avoid this happening if possible. We can ask Saul to have a word with him. They are good friends."

***

Brendan sat in the back of the truck wondering where he would end up. He was not scared. Something about the men and their attitude suggested that he was not being transported to his death. He hoped he was going to see Mary-Jane.

The truck stopped outside a small cottage near Epping Forest. Brendan saw no reason to try to escape. His first thought was always about Mary-Jane's welfare.

He was marched into the cottage and told to sit down and not move. He waited for hours. The guards were outside, talking quietly. They spoke German so Brendan could not understand what they were saying. However, he did hear Mary-Jane's name mentioned.

Brendan had nodded off while waiting. He awoke when he heard a commotion outside. The door opened. He was ordered to stand to attention by a guard. The baron entered. He was dressed in a business suit. He looked around the room.

"Are you being treated well, Sergeant Major?"

"Yes, Herr Baron. Very well."

"Good, you will stay here until you are next needed. If you cooperate and do not cause irritation, I may have a surprise for you."

He turned his back on Brendan and said to the lead guard, "If he is troublesome, shoot him and bury the body outside."

He walked out of the cottage. Brendan did not see him for another month.

***

DI Jonas Smethwick and DS Archie Routledge were awaiting the arrival of Arthur Middleton. A meeting had been arranged to discuss the conspiracy case.

Arthur entered the room accompanied by a stranger dressed in formal wear. Arthur introduced him as, "An interested party from the palace. I am sorry, Sergeant, I must ask you to leave. It is a matter of national security."

"Of course, sir." The DS stood up and left the room.

"Is that really necessary, Arthur?" Jonas asked.

"Sorry, instructions from a higher authority."

Jonas continued. "So far, we have been unable to find the suspects, Cartney, Mizel, also known as Switzer. Our inside man, Brendan O'Carroll, is missing, presumed dead. Before O'Carroll went missing, he told us that the main plotters were Baron von Marburg, his office manager, only known as the 'Hauptmann', two police officers, Silas Maitland, and Gerald Graham. We know that they are leading figures in the Irish rebel movement and active in the Friends of Hibernia. Up to now, the trail has gone cold. Our informers in rebel circles know nothing. Intelligence from tabs on the anarchist community is equally sparse."

"If I may, gentleman?" the man from the palace interjected. "You do not appear to have any worthwhile information, at present. I cannot go back to his…" Here he stopped and said, "My general, and tell him we are unable to stop possibly the most serious threat to the nation in many years."

Arthur fidgeted uncomfortably. "Sir, I have some good news. We received this information earlier today. I wanted to have it checked before informing you."

"Please go on."

"Baron von Marburg entered the country yesterday morning. An officer of the customs service recognised him from a description the special branch sent to the ports. We have been tailing him since he left the port."

"Well done, Arthur." Jonas was smiling broadly.

"Yes, well done, Superintendent. Or perhaps we should congratulate the customs officer, for being alert. At least I can take back a little good news. If you value your jobs, gentlemen, you will not lose the suspect."

He stood up, placed his top hat on his head and waited before the door. Arthur took the hint and opened it.

"Archie, get in here," Jonas said.

"I did not want to say anymore in front of the colonel, but we may have found O'Carroll too," Arthur said.

"Alive?"

"It is possible. Our officer saw a tall man in a cottage which the baron visited. He said the man was being guarded by three or four others. They all had a military bearing."

"What can we do to help?" Jonas asked.

"Nothing at present. The baron is staying in Essex, in a hotel. He is guarded by at least a platoon of fit men. I would, however, like to take your DS."

"Why?"

"We have noticed that the cottage gets daily deliveries

from a local shop. I would like Archie to take them over. We need someone who can fit in, but also has the intelligence to pick up on any information."

"Well, Sergeant, what do you say? Do you want to join special branch, albeit temporarily?"

"Anything to help, sir."

"Good, we will transport you to the village. You will be the shopkeeper's cousin from London. He is ex-army, and more than willing to help us," Arthur said.

Archie Routledge settled into village life. The shopkeeper, Samuel Smith, introduced Archie to his customers. In the afternoon, Sam took him on his rounds, to those who were living outside the village or were elderly.

"This is Paddy. He is eight years old. I've had him since he was a colt. If you want to get to know him, always have an apple spare. He'll be your friend for life," Samuel said as he patted Paddy's neck.

When they arrived at the cottage where Brendan was being held, Sam introduced Archie to the leader of the men. He was friendly but stared at Archie without blinking. As soon he was sure that Archie was not a threat, he relaxed a little.

"Nice to meet you. We will see you every day. How long are you staying?"

"I hope to stay as long as Sam needs me. It's much nicer here than London. The people are friendly. I could see myself living out my life here."

The man looked at Archie, smiled and said, "Good." He turned and called a colleague. "Take the food to the kitchen."

Sam and Archie returned to the cart and drove off at a quiet pace. Neither man said anything.

Twenty-Four

Archie

Brendan knew that a new man had taken over delivering the food. He heard him talking outside. He was convivial and laughed with the guards.

After the first week, Archie was trusted enough to put the groceries on the kitchen table. Once a week, the guards paid the account in full.

Whenever he was in the cottage, Archie would scan the premises, always looking for a sign of Brendan. There was none.

On Saturday, Archie was approaching the cottage and noticed a carriage outside. It was obvious that it was a gentlemen. He also noticed that one of the guards was intently looking at him.

When he arrived at the cottage, the guard walked toward him.

"Leave the food by the door. I will put it away later."

Archie did as he was told. He waited. The guard said, "Well?"

Archie replied, "It's Saturday; the account?"

"Wait here."

Archie moved towards the cottage, ostensibly checking the flowers. He looked through the window and saw a well-dressed gentleman. The other guards stood to attention.

Before him stood Brendan. He was dishevelled. His hair was unkempt. His hands were bound. His head was lowered as if he was being told off.

"What are you doing there?" the guard shouted.

"Nothing, just admiring your flowers."

A shout was heard from inside the cottage. He grabbed Archie by the arm and pulled him into the cottage.

"Who is this?" the baron asked.

"It is the delivery man, Herr Baron."

Brendan had been pushed toward the kitchen table. His hands were hidden from view.

"What is your name?"

"Archie, sir."

"Well, Archie, do you usually look through windows on your rounds?"

"Sorry, sir, force of habit. There are several elderly customers to visit. I usually look through the window just to make sure that they are safe. Sam, my boss, is adamant that we have to look after each other."

"Do you know this man?" The baron pointed at Brendan.

"No, sir, never met him."

"And you, Sergeant Major, do you know this man?"

Brendan recognised him. "No, Herr Baron, I have never seen him before."

The baron studied each man's face and demeanour. Nothing was said for a long time.

"This man is a bad man. We have arrested him for heinous crimes. His friends are trying to free him. This I cannot allow. You understand?"

"Yes, sir, I understand," Archie said.

"We will only need the food for another week. If no one tries to free him before I can take him to meet his accusers, I will give you five pounds as a thank you."

"You have my word, sir," Archie replied.

"Good, you may go."

Archie walked out slowly, boarded the cart, and left at a sedate pace.

"When I leave, he should have an accident."

"Yes, Herr Baron," The lead guard said.

"Sergeant Major, if you try to escape again, Mary-Jane will disappear. You will never see her or know where she is buried. Do I make myself clear?"

After the baron had left the cottage, one of the guards changed into a boiler suit. It was black. He put on heavy army boots. He blackened his face and wore a woollen beret. He slipped out of the cottage and trailed Archie's cart.

He cut across the countryside into the woods. He knew that Archie had three drops after the cottage visit. All the customers were elderly and lived on the borders of Epping Forest.

Archie, as instructed by Sam, stopped at a crossroad, to allow the pony to rest for ten minutes. Archie got the feed bag out and fixed it to the pony's muzzle. It happily munched on its hay. Archie had an apple as a treat for the beast.

He looked around and made sure it was clear. He took a small notebook from the cart. He made himself comfortable and wrote out a report of the day's happenings.

After delivering to Rose Briar Cottage, he waved goodbye to old Miss Goodwin. There was a young Miss Goodwin living there too, but she was out for the day. He continued to the next customer, three miles away.

The pony walked at a steady pace. Archie did not need to steer it; it knew where to go. He relaxed.

Something caught his eye, just on his right-hand side. Someone was following him. All he could see was a shadow. He knew that he had to go down a lane which had overgrown trees. It was quite dark, even in bright sunshine. He felt for his pistol, hidden by his feet in a box.

He guessed that one of the guards was following him. He mumbled to himself, "No crisp new fiver for me."

"Whoa." Archie stopped the pony. He climbed down from the cart and stretched. He walked toward the trees, pretending to unbutton his flies. He waited. He heard someone behind him. He turned.

A tall man dressed in black, holding a knife, was approaching him. The determination was clear on his face. Archie stood watching him. He felt for the pistol. It was comforting.

Before Archie could level the pistol, the man rushed him. Both men fell to the ground. If the assailant thought a delivery man was a soft target, he was sadly mistaken.

Archie brought his knee swiftly up to the man's groin. He felt the pain explode. He rolled off Archie, who followed up the move with a kick to the assailant's ribs. The attacker was in agony on the floor.

Archie made a simple mistake. It nearly cost him his life. Since the man was down, he pulled out his handcuffs from his coat pocket. He knelt and tried to restrain him.

The attacker was far from defeated. He wrestled with Archie and managed to pin him down. His hands went to Archie's throat. He gripped him tightly. The breath was slowly being cut off. Archie tried to pull the hands away, to no avail. He began to punch the attacker in the ribs. His grip loosened.

Archie knew he had one chance left. He brought his legs up and managed to topple his attacker. They both faced each other again. The attacker was looking around the floor for his knife. He dived for it and picked it up.

Archie felt for his pistol, it had fallen out. The attacker smiled a grim smile. "Why would a delivery man have a service pistol? I think perhaps you are not who you pretend to be. No matter. You will die today."

At that, he lunged toward Archie. The knife found its target. It caught Archie in the side of his body. He fell backwards. He grasped the lapels of the attacker's boiler suit. Bringing his legs up into the stomach of the man, he pulled back and, at the same time, pushed with his legs. The man was somersaulted over Archie's head.

The attacker was driven through the air. His knife stayed in Archie's side. He came down on his head. There was an ominous crack, as his neck gave way under the pressure. He was dead before the rest of his body had settled.

Archie lay on the ground trying to staunch his wound. He succeeded in climbing onto the cart, after some effort. "Paddy, home," he managed to say to the pony. It set off in the direction of its home. Two hours later, Paddy walked into the grocer's yard. Archie was found and taken to the village doctor.

Twenty-Five
The Skirmish

Arthur Middleton heard about the attempted murder of Archie Routledge. He and Jonas took a coach to Epping. They met Samuel and he related what he had seen.

"Mr Archie said that he saw a sergeant major in the cottage. Does that make any sense, sir?"

"Yes, thank you, Samuel. Where is Archie now?"

"He's been taken to the main hospital in Chelmsford, sir."

"Thank you again, Samuel. We will deal with the situation. Please be assured that your service to the nation will not be forgotten."

"Thank you, sir. If I may, there is something else. Constable Martindale has opened an investigation into the circumstances about the accident."

"Accident?" Jonas asked.

"I told the doctor that Mr Archie had fallen from the cart

and stuck himself on a pole. I couldn't tell him that he'd been stabbed could I, sir?"

"No not really," Jonas replied.

"Have you been back to the cottage since the accident?" Arthur asked.

"Yes, sir, I had to deliver the last pieces that Mr Archie could not. I went back to the cottage the next day as usual. They seemed surprised. They asked me about Mr Archie. I told them that he'd had an accident. I told them that I did not know where or how. They appeared to believe me."

Arthur and Jonas stepped away from Samuel. "I think it would be wise to have a word with Constable Martindale. We can use his office to call for reinforcements. Our first priority is to save O'Carroll. He may have important information about the attack. Archie is in good hands."

"I agree," said Jonas. "We must find out what opposition we are likely to face. I take it the baron is under surveillance?"

"Yes, I have a team of experienced officers watching his every move."

Both officers shook Mr Smith's hand. It was a short walk to Constable Martindale's home. It also operated as his police office. The house was locked. They walked to the post office and used the telephone to call Scotland Yard. Within hours, a platoon of infantry was dispatched to Epping. They arrived in lorries, and quickly surrounded the cottage.

As night fell, a chink of light could be seen coming from the cottage. Arthur and Jonas spoke to First Lieutenant Charles Fitzwalters, who oversaw the men. Arthur told him what he needed to know. The order to move forward was given.

***

In the cottage, the three remaining guards were worried when their leader did not return. They secured Brendan to his bed with cuffs. One guard stayed to watch him. The other two went out to find their man.

It was easy to track him. They knew where he was headed. After half an hour, they came across his body. They looked around and saw the blood trail.

As they made a stretcher from their jackets and two poles fashioned from branches, Constable Martindale approached them. He had been investigating the accident area.

The two men quickly overcame him. He was being held by one while the other plunged a knife into his stomach. His body was hidden in the undergrowth. It took them over an hour to get their leader back to the cottage. Their fallen comrade was buried in a shallow grave. The remaining soldiers readied their weapons, they expected to be attacked very soon. They were on alert all night.

In the afternoon, they saw a cart and a driver coming toward the cottage. Sam greeted them amiably. The new leader asked the question that was worrying them.

"How is Archie? Will he recover?"

"I have to be truthful, sir. It does not look good. There is dirt and wood splinters in the wound. The doctor was not hopeful. We should know by tonight or tomorrow at the latest. When I come back tomorrow, I should have more news."

"Thank you, that would be most kind."

The leader watched as Sam and the cart moved away slowly. He scanned the countryside. It was quiet. Nothing stirred. He went inside and gave an order in German. The others started to barricade the windows. Tables were moved to the windows. Arms were unpacked from cases. Within an hour, the cottage resembled an armoury. If an attack came, they would be ready for it.

***

The troops moved forward slowly. They used the terrain for cover. The lieutenant used his binoculars to watch the cottage. Jonas and Arthur reluctantly sat in the officer's car; this was to be an army operation.

At first light, the lieutenant and the sergeant walked forward towards the cottage, the sergeant held a white flag.

"My God, what is he doing?" Jonas exclaimed.

"Trying to get O'Carroll out alive, I would think," Arthur replied.

"They will get themselves killed," Jonas said.

"Maybe, or perhaps the occupants will see sense, who knows?"

A single shot hit the ground in front of the officer.

"So, that is the answer," Arthur said.

The officer and the sergeant turned and walked back to the army line.

"Sergeant?"

"Yes, sir?"

"You know what to do."

The sergeant took his whistle and blew three times. The platoon moved forward. Four soldiers ran forward and began to set up a Maxim machine gun. They came under fire. They returned a withering hail of fire. The bullets were hitting the wall above the door.

They had orders to avoid bloodshed if possible. The hostage was to be rescued, not killed by his rescuers. Inside, the remaining guards were sheltering on the floor. In the bedroom, Brendan had turned over his bed and crawled under it for protection. The only orders the baron had given the leader was not to be taken; and that Brendan must not be allowed to live.

The leader crawled toward the bedroom door. The machine gun had started again. The bullets were now a little lower. Anyone standing up would have been killed instantly.

There was a pause in the firing, the leader took the opportunity to enter the bedroom. He saw the overturned bed. He smiled. He released his pistol and fired three shots into the mattress. He moved forward to look at his handiwork. At that moment, the machine gun started again. He was hit several times and fell onto the bed.

Brendan knew that he was not destined to come out of this dangerous situation alive. However, he was a fighter. He guessed that the guards would try again to shoot him. Under the bed, he was a sitting target. He crawled out again and pulled a wardrobe next to the bed. Bullets were hitting the top of the wardrobe and shattering the wood. The noise was overwhelming.

He managed to sit in the bottom and close the doors as fully as possible. His wrist was still attached to the cuff and bed frame. He pulled a blanket and covered his wrist and arm. There was a lull in the shooting. He heard the bedroom door open, someone with heavy military boots entered. Brendan held his breath. He heard the man swear.

He pulled his comrade off the bed. It was obvious he was dead. He looked at the bed and opened fire again. At once, the machine gun fired again. He swiftly fell to the floor to avoid the gunshots.

The newcomer crawled towards the bed. Brendan felt the man pulling the blanket. A machine gun was firing at intervals. Brendan realised that this was his last chance, with the pistol he had retrieved from the dead leader, he looked through the wardrobe doors and fired one shot into the prone soldier.

The other guards made a joke about gunshots. They were sure that Brendan had been shot. After the salvo they heard one shot. Then everything went quiet. They supposed it was the kill shot.

Brendan waited for a moment. The machine gun started again. He used the distraction to get out of the wardrobe. The newcomer's head was turned toward him. His eyes were glazed over. Blood trickled from his mouth.

He pulled the body over and went through its pockets. He found the key to the cuffs and unlocked them. He took the pistol from the dead man's hand. He checked the magazine, it was empty. He checked both dead bodies for spare ammunition. He reloaded and crawled toward the door. The bullets were still hitting the cottage. Another machine gun had started from the left side. Brendan was safe as long as he stayed near to the floor.

The remaining guards were hiding behind an old sofa. They began to get worried about their comrade. When there was another lull, one shouted.

"Kurt, wo sind sie?"

He began to crawl towards the bedroom. The door slowly opened. He expected to see Kurt, but instead, Brendan was lying flat on his stomach, aiming the pistol at him. Before the soldier could react, Brendan pulled the trigger, the soldier died instantly.

The lone guard saw the prone figure of Brendan and returned fire. The guard was using a machine pistol. The bullets sprayed out hitting the floor, door, and wall, in front of Brendan who had retreated to behind the wardrobe.

Throughout the gun fight in the cottage, the infantry had moved closer. They now waited within fifty feet of their target. The machines guns were set up ready should it be necessary. A squad of men had moved toward the back of the cottage.

They had intelligence that Brendan was likely to be in the bedroom. The lieutenant had joined the sergeant undercover by the cottage. He held a megaphone. "In the cottage. My name is Lieutenant Fitzwalters. I command the men who have you surrounded. Release your hostage and we can end this unhappy affair without further bloodshed."

There was no answer from inside the cottage. Brendan had heard something but could not clearly hear what was being said. His impaired hearing, because of his artillery service, together with the bullets in a confined space, had made him almost deaf. He decided to take a chance. He screamed at the top of his voice, "I'm in the bedroom. I've killed three. Help!"

The guard took aim and fired again. Brendan crawled against the bedroom wall. The lieutenant gave the signal to the machine gunner on the left to direct fire toward the front of the cottage, from top to bottom.

The gunner opened fire. The sole surviving guard had no chance. He lay down. He could run toward the bedroom but knew that Brendan would shoot him. The bullets slowly crept down the wall. He knew that it was over. He held the muzzle of the machine pistol to his head and fired.

The sergeant shouted, "Cease fire. Smoke."

Smoke bombs were thrown into the front and bedroom windows. The smoke enveloped the cottage. Brendan's eyes were streaming, and he was coughing violently. He crawled toward the bedroom door. Passing through it, he noticed the limp form of his last attacker.

As he crawled toward the light of the front door, he saw that the ceiling was alight. With a great effort, he flung himself through the door. Immediately he was jumped on by two soldiers who tied his hands. He was marched away. Other troops entered the cottage and confirmed that the attackers had been killed.

Twenty-Six
Target Identified?

Jonas and Arthur were driven to the cottage. The lieutenant saluted smartly, "The hostage is safe. As per your orders he has been cuffed and is under guard. We found one body in a shallow grave. There are three other bodies in the cottage. One appears to have committed suicide. The weapons are German in origin. The clothes are also German military issue. Are you able to tell me what happened here?"

"I am sorry, Lieutenant, orders from above. We will be taking the hostage back to Scotland Yard. Thank you for your help. Rest assured that your help today will not be forgotten."

The platoon stayed to quell the fire that had erupted. They left when it was doused.

Brendan sat quietly in the back of the lieutenant's car, which had been loaned to Arthur to take them to the nearest train station.

"What's to happen to Mary-Jane?" Brendan enquired.

"Sergeant Major, I have already reminded you to be silent. If you do not obey my orders, I will gag you. Do I make myself clear?"

"Yes, sir. I'm just worried, sir."

Arthur was increasingly irritated by Brendan's questions. He seemed more concerned about his wife than the upcoming attack.

After many hours of travel, they finally arrived back at Scotland Yard. Brendan was placed in a cell, while Jonas and Arthur decided on the tactics. They were determined to get every drop of information they could squeeze from him.

Brendan was fed and allowed to change into an ill-fitting overall. He sat in an interrogation cell. The officer posted at the door ignored him.

Jonas and Arthur entered the cell. Jonas started the interview by warning Brendan that he was still under arrest and that unless he fully cooperated, he would be sent to a military tribunal for trial and sentence.

"I understand, sir," Brendan replied.

"We know you attacked the baron. What happened after that?" Jonas asked.

"I was taken to a boat. I do not know where it was moored. I have no idea how long I was at sea. When I awoke, I was bundled into a carriage. It was several weeks before the baron appeared. As soon as I reached a large house with high walls around it, I knew it was near the sea. I could smell it and there were seagulls crying all the time. I was beaten daily.

"They did not ask me anything at first. But, as it went on, I realised they wanted information about the anarchists.

Particularly Franz Mizel, I told them I had never met him. They showed me his photograph and I had to admit that I did recognise him. I was severely beaten for lying.

"When the baron came, he told me that I would be executed the next morning. They did that for at least two weeks. I was a bag of nerves. One day, Mary-Jane appeared. I do not know where from. They made her watch my execution. Up until that point no bullets had been fired. This time, someone made a mistake, and I was shot in the arm. The baron was furious. Mary-Jane collapsed, and I have not seen her since. I am ashamed to say I told them everything."

"Did you mention our involvement?" Arthur asked.

"No, sir, I thought that they would be satisfied with what I had told them. The baron told me I would be moved. I did not know where to. I asked him about Mary-Jane, he threatened to kill me if I spoke of her again. After another long boat trip, I was escorted to a boatyard where I was put to work. I helped them fit a machine gun to the rear of a barge. An Armstrong cannon was fitted to the front. The workers were nearly all German. I think military.

"I was then sent to the cottage. You know what happened there. I saw your sergeant. I think they killed him. They were laughing. Also, at the boatyard, I saw Franz Mizel, Liam something or other, and Sergeant Maitland."

Arthur and Jonas were particularly interested in the boatyard. They stopped the interview, while Arthur contacted his army contacts.

The interview lasted all day and into the early hours of the morning. Brendan was drained. The two inquisitors were relentless. After they had finished with him, they moved to Arthur's office.

"That barge worries me," Arthur said. "A cannon and machine gun means the attack will be very violent. A seven-pound shell can do real damage."

"What are we talking about, damage-wise?" Jonas enquired.

"That particular cannon was used in India. It usually sits atop a fort. It is a mountain cannon. It has a range of thousand yards. It was used to wipe out any invading force. If it were fired into Tower Bridge, it could damage the structure beyond repair. I hate to think if it was used against the royal yacht."

Both men sat in silence for a while.

"So, you think the target is the yacht or Tower Bridge?" Jonas asked.

"If we put all the information gleaned from O'Carroll and what we already know from our own investigation; it is obvious to me, that the king is the target. I suspect that the tenth anniversary of the construction of Tower Bridge is the date of the attack. We need to involve the palace."

There was a knock on the door, a constable entered and passed a note to Arthur. He read it and passed it to Jonas.

"It is not good news. The baron has managed to lose the tail I had on him," Arthur said.

"Perhaps he will call off the attack? He surely must know that we have O'Carroll?" Jonas asked.

"Somehow, I do not think so. It has gone too far. We need to assume that the anniversary will be the beginning."

"I agree. We need to look at the palace plans for the

day. With this new information, security will have to be increased," Jonas replied.

"That is not as easy as it sounds, the colonel, or rather, the equerry, is not enamoured with what we have done so far."

There was another knock at the door. A new message arrived. Arthur read its contents. "The boatyard has been vacated. There is no sign of the barge, or the team of workers. They have disappeared."

"Oh dear, how do we explain that to the colonel?" Jonas sighed.

"Nevertheless, we need to visit the palace," Arthur said.

**

Franz and Saul met to discuss the attack details. Franz began by asking about security.

"Saul, are you completely happy with the security of the project?"

"Overall, yes, although I am concerned that we are not being fully briefed about the details of the attack."

"Is Raul open to your questions?"

Saul thought for a moment. "Sometimes, I am not sure that he is working for us. He went off with Udo on a secret assignment. He refused to tell me why. He got very agitated."

"Ah, yes, Udo. What do you think about our steersman?"

"I do not trust him. Why do we need so many Germans in the plan?"

"Saul, I need you to do something for me."

"What do you need?"

"I have my suspicions about the German influence in the plan. Did you see the barge when it was finished? It could take on a battleship. This is not the plan we put together. I think we have been used again to further German interests. If that is so, our revolution may be of secondary interest to our backers. We must find out before the attack starts. You must speak to Raul. Find out who our backers are. Be insistent with him. If necessary, use force. We have one month left. Can you do that?"

"You do not trust him?"

"I do not," replied Franz.

"Leave it to me."

"Saul, be careful, I am being followed, and not by the authorities."

***

Saul had known Raul for over ten years. He liked him, but deep down, he questioned his commitment to the revolution. He felt that he was a dilettante. He was sure that Raul was not a traitor, although he had questions about the money he had and how he came by it. Raul was a self-confessed thief, but Saul thought that he must be an extraordinary professional to always have money and never arrested once since he had known him.

Saul tried to tail him after a meeting, but Raul lost him very quickly. He realised that he needed help. He recruited two anarchists who had no knowledge of the plot or Raul Santiago.

The four main plotters were meeting regularly at the

Covent Garden address. Franz, Liam, and Saul were careful not to mention their doubts about the banker.

All went smoothly. After their usual meal, they left the meeting at intervals. Liam went first. Within minutes he had disappeared into the back streets. Saul went next. He met up with the two anarchists. They waited for Raul.

Raul came out and looked up and down the road. He buttoned his coat and walked off quickly. Saul pointed at Raul. The two men nodded and began to follow him at a distance. They separated and followed him, always keeping well back.

Raul knew that something was wrong. Call it sixth sense. He decided to slow down and walk around the West End. The crowds were pushing and shoving as they went about their business.

He soon detected one follower. He walked toward Charing Cross station. When he arrived at the concourse, he went into the gentleman's toilet. He waited for a few minutes and left again.

The man followed him out of the toilets. Raul took the steps down to the river. His 'shadow' followed. The poorest people had set up home in the surrounding area. Beggars accosted anyone dressed smartly.

Raul gave a beggar a coin. He was surrounded by a noisy crowd hoping for more. He used the disturbance to slip away. He ran through the arches below the station and appeared in the Strand.

He jumped on a bus heading for Waterloo Bridge. He was confident that he had lost the 'tail'. He sat back and relaxed.

Saul's second agent had waited on the opposite pavement in front of Charing Cross station. He suspected that the station was a diversion. The little information Saul had been able to give him suggested that Raul habitually crossed Waterloo Bridge to get home.

After ten minutes, he saw Raul run across the Strand to a bus stop. He nonchalantly took his place in the queue. He ignored Raul and settled on the top floor. He had a clear view of anyone getting on or off. The bus travelled across Waterloo Bridge and headed toward York Road. Raul alighted the bus and walked in the direction of Westminster Bridge. His tail stayed on one stop further and got off. He looked back and saw Raul hail a cab.

The cab passed him. Luckily, Saul had given the man enough money for every contingency. He hailed his own cab and told the cabbie to follow the one in front. Raul usually changed cabs before going home, but he was confident that he had left his tail by the river. The second cab stopped, one hundred yards away from Raul's. It had stopped outside a three-storey town house, on Brixton Hill.

Raul entered the premises. The watcher dismissed the cab, found a doorway opposite the house, and waited. In the morning, the watcher decided that this was Raul's home address.

Later that morning, Saul thanked the man for his diligence and passed him a five-pound note.

Twenty-Seven

Questions

Jonas and Arthur entered the palace via the tradesman's entrance. A corporal escorted them to a room off the barracks. They entered and were astonished to see a large conference table. Those seated were evidently waiting for them to arrive.

The colonel rose. "Now that we are all here, we can begin."

Introductions were given only if a member spoke. Jonas was feeling small and intimidated by the throng. It was clear that these were members of the king's retinue, civil servants and the highest ranks of the army and navy.

The colonel said, "Gentlemen, His Majesty will not change the itinerary for the fourth. He has been assured by the Kaiser of no ill intent toward the royal family. I wish I had His Majesty's confidence. The news from Superintendent Middleton and Inspector Smethwick is, frankly, chilling. Their report is in appendix IV. Although we cannot cancel the celebrations, I believe we can ensure that these anarchists and fellow travellers do not get near enough to His Majesty and the royal family to harm them."

The colonel paused to allow the gravity of the situation to sink in.

"Superintendent, would you bring the meeting up to date?"

"Thank you, sir. The inspector and I are now concentrating on finding Baron von Marburg, and the anarchist ringleaders. Liam Cartney and Franz Mizel—"

"It says in your report that you had the baron under surveillance and then lost him," a senior army officer interrupted Arthur.

"Please, Sir Edward, allow the inspector to continue," the colonel said.

"Seems shoddy, to allow a suspect to get away, under your nose, as it were," Sir Edward retorted.

Sir Edward was not placated. "Why are civilians here? This is a military matter. We will blow them out of the water. Death's too good for them…"

Sir Edward continued criticising everyone and everything. It took the colonel time to get back control of the meeting.

"Please go on, Superintendent."

"Our informant, who worked on the barge, has given us a detailed description of the arms to be used. Of greatest concern is a cannon. I am told that it fires a seven-pound projectile; capable of throwing a shell four thousand yards. They have a Maxim machine gun, able to fire two hundred and fifty rounds a minute. The gunwale has been fitted with iron plate. We believe that thirty men could fire through the slots. We cannot allow that barge to get anywhere near the celebrations."

"Thank you, Superintendent. Inspector, what are the police doing to find the baron and his anarchists?"

"From my interrogation of our informant, Brendan O'Carroll, I believe this attack will be less about creating a revolution, more about an invasion by Germany."

The room stirred. The dignitaries were feeling uncomfortable.

"That is extraordinary. Whatever gave you that idea?" a senior civil servant asked.

"Our informer trained the workmen. He was of the opinion that they were all military, German military. We know that the baron told O'Carroll to get as much information he could about Franz Mizel, the leading anarchist. Why would the German military help European anarchists unless it was a ploy to use them? These men have fled the continent. Many are wanted by the German authorities. It does not make sense. If I am correct, I intend to concentrate on finding Mizel. My intention is to turn him against the baron. If it works, we may be able to stop the attack before it gets anywhere near the king."

"The truth is, Inspector, it will be our task to stop an attack taking place. What makes you think you can find him, when, and do forgive me, you have failed so far?"

"I intend to free O'Carroll. It will not be long before he finds the conspirators again. They have his wife. He will be very determined."

"Admiral, what plans do you have to deal with the barge?" the colonel asked.

"Simple really, I will have a cruiser stationed at Dagenham. I will have patrol boats from the Pool of London to the cruiser and beyond. The barge cannot get near His Majesty."

The colonel smiled. "Thank you, gentlemen, we will meet again in a week, when I hope to have good news." Here he looked at Jonas and Arthur.

***

Saul, Liam, and Franz absorbed the evidence concerning Raul. They sat in the Covent Garden address, by the fire.

"You are sure about the address?" Liam asked.

"I'm sure," Saul replied.

"That would explain how Raul was able to disappear for long periods. He is obviously working for someone outside our circle of comrades," Franz said.

"I cannot believe he is a traitor." Liam was adamant.

"It would also explain the money. None of us ever pressed him about his finances. His little presents for the meetings must have cost quite a penny. We all sat back and took his largesse, without a murmur."

Saul stood by the fire and warmed his hands. "If he has gone over to the enemy, this address is compromised. Whoever he is working for will know all our haunts, friends, and plans."

"The authorities could be outside, waiting to arrest us," Liam said.

"I do not believe it is the authorities we need worry about," Franz said. He continued. "We have all noticed that the German contingent has grown. Our original plan has diminished. It was Raul who got the finances. It was Raul who introduced Udo. Now, it seems, that Udo is running the whole affair. We have been pushed to the background. No, I believe Raul is working for German interests."

"Intelligence or the military?" Liam asked.

"From our perspective, it does not matter. Either one is the enemy of the revolution," Saul said.

Liam was not convinced. "We need to confront Raul. If he comes clean, perhaps we can regain the initiative."

"Raul is a strong individual. It will not be easy to confront him. What if he denies everything? Do we torture him to get the truth? We do not know what the truth is. What do you think, Franz?" Saul said.

"I think that to have Raul against us would be very bad. He is formidable. He is always armed. As to torture, who would do it? I personally find it distasteful. But I have been involved in it the past."

"I will do if it, if you think it will get to the truth." Saul said.

"I am not sure. Raul is a comrade. We have no evidence against him, apart from living in a house, it may have been an assignation. Could we follow him some more?" Liam pleaded.

"We need to agree on the next step. Time is short," Franz said.

Saul looked at Liam. "We cannot act, unless we all agree."

"Ask him. Torture, as a last resort."

***

At Scotland Yard, Brendan O'Carroll sat in a cell awaiting his fate. He suspected that his usefulness to the authorities was over and that Middleton's threat to have him hanged was likely to happen.

The cell door opened, and Jonas and Arthur entered. The constable left the room.

"Well, Sergeant Major, it appears that the baron has abandoned you," Arthur said.

Brendan was resigned to his fate. "What will happen to me now, sir?"

"You will hang for your crimes. What else would you expect. You are a traitor, a murderer and thief," Arthur said.

"I have helped you, sir. Surely that should help my case. I fear the rope. Please, sir, allow me to die as a soldier?"

"Soldiers do not train enemies to use British cannons," Jonas said, with venom in his voice.

"I had to, sir. They would have killed Mary-Jane."

There was silence in the room, as each man mulled over what had been said.

"I believe you met the gentleman known as 'Franz Mizel'? Is that correct?"

"Yes, sir. I was taken to a flat near Covent Garden market. They blindfolded me, but it was obvious where I was. The smells, shouts of the traders and the crowds. He was not introduced, but I heard one of the men call him Franz. The other main man was called 'Raul', both foreigners."

Arthur spoke to Jonas, both ignored Brendan. "If we could find out where that flat was, perhaps we could arrest the foreigner; what do you think?"

"It is possible, although we would need someone to help us," Jonas replied.

Brendon realised that they were offering an opening. "I can, sir. I can show you where the flat is."

"Do you think he can be trusted?" Arthur asked Jonas.

"Personally, I would not trust him at all," Jonas said.

"I swear, sir, on Mary-Jane's life. I will help you."

***

The baron had fled his hotel near Epping Forest when he had overheard a tradesman gossiping about an army convoy heading toward the forest.

He suspected that the hideout had been found. He had confidence that his men would not surrender or be taken prisoner. O'Carroll would be killed if they were attacked.

His carriage took him to Woolwich free ferry, where he crossed over to Greenwich. He stopped at two anonymous hostels, one on each side of the river, to break his journey.

His goal was to get to Erith Marshes, where the barge lay hidden. The baron would check that everything was ready, then return to Germany to await the outcome of his plan.

Twenty-Eight

Unlikely Alliance

Brendan was allowed to walk around Covent Garden to get his bearings. The market had been discreetly surrounded by police officers; all the entrances covered.

Arthur watched Brendan as he inspected each building. After two hours, Brendan stopped in front of a building. It looked much the same as every other one, however, he was sure.

Without waiting for permission, he strode to the top floor. Arthur and Jonas waited outside for him. Brendan knocked on the door. He remembered a sequence of taps. The door slowly opened a little. Franz looked out at Brendan.

"Sergeant Major, what are you doing here?" Franz was concerned and kept eyeing the stairs.

"I am alone," Brendan said. "Baron von Marburg is paying me to spy on you."

"You had better come in and tell me what has happened."

Brendan told Franz the story that Arthur and Jonas had concocted. It had elements of truth, interspersed with lies. The story told of the anarchists being used by German intelligence to discredit the anarchist movement in England and the continent. The blame for the outrage would lay at the feet of Franz and his co-conspirators. It was just enough to throw doubt into the mix.

"Why are you telling me this, Sergeant Major? The baron would certainly have you killed if he found out."

"He has my wife. He abducted her and is holding her. I want your help to rescue her."

"I see." Franz had a healthy suspicion of those offering him help. What did the sergeant major want in return?

"And if I help you, what will you do for me?"

"Anything you want, sir," Brendan replied.

"Will you kill the baron?"

"I will."

"Are you alone, Sergeant Major? Perhaps you have the authorities waiting for me?"

"No, sir, I am a wanted man. I will hang if I am taken."

Franz went to the window and looked out at the market. He studied it for a few minutes. Nothing appeared out of place.

"Do you have somewhere to hide, Sergeant Major?"

"Yes, sir, I know the city very well. There is a warehouse near Puddle Dock, in the basement. It is not used. I have a key."

"Go there. Wait until I send someone to get you. It will not be long. Then we will get your wife."

Franz waited until midnight to leave the premises. He

walked around, doubled back, and did everything to lose any tail. He eventually arrived at his destination.

Liam and Saul sat in the last row of pews. St Matthew's Church was holding a service. In truth, the priest had opened the church to accommodate the poor and needy. The nights were always cold for those without proper clothing or hungry.

Franz joined the others. He told them everything Brendan had said. They discussed their next options. After hearing the story, Liam volunteered to help Saul find the truth from Raul.

Saul and Liam waited outside the Brixton address on Sunday morning. Raul exited the house and started to walk toward the Oval. Liam was astonished by Raul's dress. He was clad in tails and a top hat. He carried a cane, which was for show rather than any infirmity.

He hailed a cab. The pair followed in their cab. A sympathiser, who owned a cab, was brought in to help them. They followed Raul, who travelled to Hyde Park. He stopped at a vendor for his favourite drink, a ginger beer. His demeanour was that of a well-to-do gentleman enjoying the morning sun.

In reality, Raul was discreetly looking at all the others strolling. He was waiting for a contact. He was surprised to see the baron walking toward him.

They both tipped their hats; this was supposed to look like a chance meeting. The Hauptmann stood behind the baron.

"Herr Baron, this is unexpected. I thought I was to meet a courier." Raul was feeling nervous.

"I will be leaving England later today. I have inspected the barge. All is well. I have decided to change the plan a little. The anarchists and the Friends of Hibernia are no longer part of the operation. You will remove them. Mizel and the others are to be eliminated. Do you understand?"

"Of course, Herr Baron. May I ask why?"

"You may not. Suffice it to say, that I have got intelligence that is worrying."

"I will need help."

The baron looked toward the Hauptmann, who walked forward. He retrieved a letter from the briefcase he was carrying. He passed it to Raul and walked away.

"That letter has the whereabouts of the FoH contingent, the sergeant major's wife and the police sergeants. The sergeant major is missing, presumed arrested. I will deal with him later. Do not fail. Herr Santiago. When you have completed your task, you will join the crew for the attack on the enemy."

"Yes, Herr Baron."

The baron walked away without acknowledging Raul.

Liam and Saul saw the encounter. Neither one recognised the man Raul had spoken to. They waited by their cab. Raul walked towards the road.

A cab pulled up in front of him, he moved forward to open the door. He saw that it was occupied, "I beg your pardon, I thought this cab was free."

He stepped back. At the same time, Saul greeted his friend, "Raul, what a surprise. Please join us."

Raul moved back; he was unsure of what to do. It was decided for him when he saw the pistol that Saul held. He climbed in, removing his top hat.

"Liam, please go through Raul's pockets."

"I am sorry. The quicker you answer the questions, the sooner this will be over."

"This is an outrage. What have I done to deserve this?" Raul said.

Liam found the letter and passed it over to Saul. Liam produced his own weapon as Saul began to read the letter. He passed it back to Liam.

"This is a warrant for our execution. Were you going to do it? I have known you for over ten years, it seems you are not the man I thought you were."

"It is not what you think. I am a double agent for the communist party. The man who gave me the letter is an enemy. I was told to get near to him and get intelligence about his plans. Franz knows all about it."

"Franz knows? Why were we kept in the dark?"

"That man has had you marked for execution since before the operation was confirmed. He is German military intelligence. He calls himself Rutger Muller. He is very dangerous. Why would I betray you? You know me. I have been protecting you. He wanted to kill you, but I told him you were central to the plan. I would die for the revolution; you know that."

"Hans, drive to the warehouse," Saul said to the driver. "Raul, I so want to believe you. But your attire and the house you are living in is well beyond the funds of a revolutionary; even an expert thief," Saul continued.

"It is my cover. The house, the clothes, are not mine. I need to appear as someone of means. I am a thief, and a good one."

Liam sat back in the cab. He wanted to believe Raul. But he had the evidence in his hand, the letter.

"Raul, please hand over your pistol," Saul said, pointing his own at his chest.

"You cannot. It is my only defence against the enemy."

"Have no fear, Raul. I will protect you," Saul said.

Raul pushed aside his jacket and removed the pistol from his waistband. He handed it to Saul.

"Sorry," said Liam.

Twenty-Nine
Raul Questioned

A young lad turned up at the Covent Garden address with a message from Saul. Franz gave the messenger a ha'penny for his troubles. He armed himself with a pistol.

He then took a cab to various places in the city. Each time he would walk for five minutes then hail a cab. When he arrived at Puddle Dock, he was confident that no one was following him.

The sergeant major heard the cab stop outside his hideout. He waited until he heard Franz calling his name. They walked to Blackfriars Bridge and hailed another cab to a warehouse on the south side of the river.

Raul was sitting in an office of a derelict warehouse. Saul and Liam were watching him. Someone knocked on the warehouse door. Saul went to open it; his gun was held ready for use.

"Is he saying anything?" Franz asked.

"Nothing. He is waiting for you."

Saul took Franz aside and asked him about the claim that Raul was an agent for the communist party. Franz smiled and said, "This is the first time I have heard this."

"Franz, what madness is this?" Raul asked as soon as he saw him.

"Hello, Raul. I am sure we can sort this out, very easily." Franz smiled.

"The man you met today…?"

"Rutger Muller, he is from German intelligence. I told the others."

"Yes, Rutger Muller, I see. What part does he play in our plan?"

"He financed it. I was to kill him after he paid us. But you wanted more."

"So, you are working for the party, are you?"

"Yes, of course. They knew that your operation was in jeopardy. They approached me to protect you. I could not tell you. It was too dangerous."

"I see, that seems plausible. However, why would the communist party want to protect an anarchist operation? Many party members despise us and would be pleased to see us murdered?"

"We both want the same thing, a revolution of the people."

"Who is Baron von Marburg?"

"I have no idea." The first signs of worry appeared on Raul's brow.

"Liam, please bring in our friend."

Brendan O'Carroll joined the group. "Sergeant Major, do you know this man?"

Brendan looked towards Raul. "Yes, sir. He brought me to meet you."

"And at any other time?"

"I saw him talking to the baron, at the dry dock. He was with the baron, his aide, the Hauptmann, and a senior military man."

"Do you know who the military man was?"

"Not his name, but I heard the baron call him Herr General."

"Thank you, Sergeant Major, please go with Liam. He will look after you."

Saul had moved behind Raul. As O'Carroll left the room, he pinioned Raul's arms behind the chair he was seated on. Franz moved quickly and tied Raul to the chair.

Franz's demeanour changed. "You will tell me everything I want to know. If you do not, I will torture you, until you do."

Raul struggled but said nothing.

Franz nodded to Saul. He brought a hammer down on Raul's right hand. The scream echoed throughout the warehouse.

"My friend, that is only a taste of what is to come."

"Fools, idiots. You are doomed. You play at revolution. You have been used since the beginning. I do not help fools," Raul raged at his attackers.

Franz nodded again to Saul, who brought the hammer down on Raul's left hand. His eyes bulged and the sweat poured from his brow.

He started to laugh. "Go ahead. I have been tortured by the best in Europe. You cannot break me. I will never give in."

He then broke into a catalogue of profanities. Franz and Saul were shocked, not by the swearing, but by the language…it was German.

Could Raul be a German? They looked at him. He had paused in his tirade.

"What is your real name?" Franz asked.

Raul did not answer. Saul lifted the hammer and brought it down on Raul's knee. The knee cracked loudly. Raul screamed. More cussing.

"What is your name?" Franz persisted.

"It will not help you," Raul managed to say. The pain was excruciating. His hands were swelling, and his knee was showing blood through his trousers.

"Saul, will you bring my bag from the office, please?"

As Saul went to the office, Franz leant over and whispered to Raul.

"My friend, you are dead. Whatever happens you will not live beyond today. I will have the information I need. I can make it easy for you or hard. You know that everyone breaks. Make it easy on yourself. Give me what I want."

Raul swung his head to the side and managed to hit Franz in the nose. It immediately started to bleed. Franz retrieved his handkerchief to wipe the blood. Raul started to laugh.

Saul saw what had happened and punched Raul in the face. He then helped Franz tend to his nose.

Franz washed his hands under a standing tap and dried himself. He held his hand out for the bag. Opening it, he brought out a small knife. Very sharp, the blade had been honed to a point. He examined it and walked toward Raul.

"Where were you born?"

He did not say anything.

"You know I have travelled the world. I've been to Spain. I know the language and people. So why, when I break your bones, do you cuss in German? A true Spaniard would surely swear in his native language."

Raul looked at Franz with hatred. "I'll never betray my country."

"I understand, but what country would that be? Saul, please go and see how our comrades are."

He nodded and walked toward the office where Liam and Brendan were. As Saul walked away, he heard a bestial cry. He did not look around. He heard Franz say, "You can stop this if you tell me everything. This is just the start."

"Never!" Raul shouted.

Liam and Brendan had heard the screams but had stayed put. Saul entered the room looking shocked. This was his best friend who had been there for him when his babies had been sick. He had paid for Agnes to see a doctor.

"What's happening?" Liam asked.

"He's a German. We think Raul is not his real name."

"What? Are you sure?" Liam said.

At that moment, another scream rang around the warehouse. Liam had tears in his eyes.

"We have to stop this," he pleaded.

Saul had taken a seat and was trying to light his pipe. He was shaking. "It's no use. Franz is determined to find the truth, whatever the consequences. Raul has betrayed us at every step. The Germans know all of our plans."

"Sergeant Major, please help. Speak to Franz, I'm begging you."

Brendan got up and looked outside. Another scream was heard more pitiful than the last.

When there was a lull, they re-entered the room. They saw Raul tied to the chair; he was blooded but still alive. Franz was checking the bonds to make sure they were tight. He looked at the newcomers. He had a determined look on his face. They knew not to disagree with his actions.

"I know you are a German. I do not like Germans. They killed my wife and child in front of me. Slit their throats. My wife first, then my baby. I cannot get at those responsible, but I have you."

"Ah, yes. The story. How many times have we heard you recite the tale of your family's death? Saul, what story did he tell you? Perhaps it was the one about being unable to get to them in time. Liam, did he tell you a comrade had informed on him and where his family was hiding?

"The truth is not so heroic, is it Franz? Why not tell them the truth? No, I shall then. Franz knew that his family was in danger, a comrade had told him. He had two days to get home and get them away. It should have taken a day. He even had the use of a horse.

"Instead, he stopped at an inn where he spent the next two days drinking and whoring. When his wife was being tortured and abused, he was in a whore's bed sleeping the grog off."

"Is this true, Franz?" Liam asked.

"No, my friend. He is trying to make us suspect each other."

"The question is, how does he know so such much about where you were when your family was taken?" Saul said.

"Yes, Raul, how do you know about the death of my family?" Franz has moved a little closer.

"I captured an officer who had taken part in an interrogation of a comrade's family. I did not know it was you. I was in Freiburg getting intelligence for our group. You could have removed your family to France in a day. Was the whore worth it?"

Franz lost his temper and dragged the knife across Raul's chest. It was a deep cut, but not deep enough to harm him too seriously. Raul was shaking all over. His head dropped. The pain had caused him to faint. Saul stepped forward and slapped him. Liam brought a bucket of water. Saul poured the water over Raul's head.

Liam walked out of the room, unable to take the sight of someone he thought was a friend. Raul's story had shaken him. He had only known Franz less than three years. He had, up until then, had confidence in Franz. Brendan stayed. He wanted to know about Mary-Jane. Within two hours, Raul was finished. Franz was right. Everyone has a limit.

Brendan watched the torture with disinterest. "Please ask him about Mary-Jane." Franz agreed.

"We will rescue your wife, Sergeant Major, I lost my 'Mary-Jane' you shall not lose yours."

They had the address of where she was being held. Raul had also come clean about the plot and the main characters.

"What shall we do with him?" Saul asked.

"You go and check on Liam. He seems to be unwell. I will take care of Raul. I will get the sergeant major to help me dispose of the body."

Saul looked at Raul, who lifted his head. Their eyes locked. Raul found no pity in his friend's eyes.

"Sergeant Major, there is an old canvas tent by the office. Please bring it."

When O'Carroll came back, Raul's body was on the floor. He had a gash across his throat. Brendan and Franz rolled the body into the tent. They weighed it down with rocks. Later it was thrown into the Thames.

Thirty
Anarchists Taken

Arthur Middleton was shocked to read in the *Telegraph*, that Buckingham Palace had announced that the king and queen would be present to mark the tenth anniversary of the opening of Tower Bridge.

It went on, 'The royal yacht *Victoria and Albert*, will moor in the Pool of London. The Royal family will host a banquet for selected guests in the evening.'

"Damn," he exclaimed.

He rushed to the office that Jonas had been given for the duration of the investigation.

"Have you seen this?" He held the paper out.

"Indeed, I have. Why release the news now?"

"Who knows? But this leaves us little time to stop the attack and arrest the culprits."

***

Liam and Saul headed to the Covent Garden flat. Brendan and Franz determined to check out the address where Mary-Jane was being held. They arrived at a building near Wapping.

The building was like every other building in the vicinity. It had seen better days. The main entrance was open to anyone. On each floor a half railing allowed light in. The stairs were made of stone. The building had lines of washing hanging from the windows and from the railings. The washing lines were fixed to the building opposite. Everyone in the block used the lines.

An old lady was putting her wet washing through an old mangle. O'Carroll approached her. After a discussion, he returned to Franz.

"She is upstairs, on the fourth floor. Two foreigners are with her."

"All right, Sergeant Major, we will return tonight and take her."

"Thank you, sir."

***

Arthur Middleton was annoyed that Brendan had been able to disappear so easily. His watchers had lost him after he had been to Franz's flat.

In response, he and Jonas had flooded the area around the flat with plain-clothed officers.

After two days, they saw Liam and another person enter the flat. Inside, Saul wiped his hands. There still was blood on them. Liam ran into the passage, where the communal toilet was, and threw up.

After many hours, Franz and Brendan arrived back. Arthur and Jonas briefed the officers. They waited until the lights went off in the flat. They delayed their entrance another half an hour. Arthur and Jonas led four armed officers.

They quietly walked up the stairs. Jonas gently pushed the door, it was locked. The biggest officer stepped back and, on Arthur's mark, barged the door open.

The officers ran in, quickly spreading out. They shouted, "Armed police". The occupants were taken by surprise. Saul tried to get to his pistol, Jonas fired, and he fell to the ground.

Liam had tried to get out of a window but stopped when he saw the drop. All of them were arrested. Brendan allowed himself to be taken. He said nothing to the officer. He looked at Jonas and then Arthur without acknowledging them.

Franz was composed. He looked at Saul, who was being tended by an officer. He saw the officer nod his head in the negative. Saul was dead. In the police station, Franz, Brendan and Liam, were put in separate cells.

"Who first?" asked Arthur.

"I think we can leave the sergeant major to stew a little. I suggest Liam. He is the weak link, in my opinion."

"Not Franz?"

"No. He is obviously the leader of this pack of miscreants. No, Liam. He is our man." Jonas was sure.

Liam sat in his cell, nervously pulling at his fingers. His breathing was fast.

Jonas entered the cell first. "Liam Cartney, or would you prefer Terrence Nightingale?"

"I have no idea who you are talking about. My name is Father Edmund Halleron. I was staying with a friend. I have no idea why I have been arrested."

"Bravo!" Jonas smiled.

"Really, officer. I am on a sabbatical in London. I have done nothing wrong. You can check with my diocese."

Jonas opened a file and began to read. "Liam Cartney, thirty-eight years old. Born in Donegal, Ireland. Trained to be a priest at Dublin seminary. Left soon after being ordained. Wanted for gunrunning for the Fenian Brotherhood. Involved in the robbery of arms in Woolwich. Known anarchist. I could go on, but it is pointless. The photograph may be old but it's you, no doubt. I have you now and no jiggery-pokery will save you."

At that moment, Arthur entered the room, in the full uniform of a superintendent.

"Has he confessed yet?"

"No, sir. He denies being Liam Cartney."

"He does, does he? Constable, please leave the room. Inspector, have you told him about the attack?"

"No, sir, I thought I would allow you to," Jonas replied.

"Excellent, you are going to the Tower of London unless you come clean about the proposed attack on His Majesty. You may be able to save yourself."

"Inspector, what happens to traitors?"

"They are hanged, sir."

"One last chance, Cartney. Tell me about the attack; when it is happening, and the forces involved?"

"I am not Liam Cartney. My name is…"

"Do not waste my time. Inspector, bring our friend in."

Jonas left the room and returned with an older gentleman, holding a briefcase. Jonas now took over the interview.

"Professor, please put your equipment on the desk. Have you heard of 'fingerprinting', Cartney? It has revolutionised detecting crime. The professor is an expert. He was one of the first men to perfect it."

"I want a solicitor," Cartney demanded.

"Sorry, you are out of luck. You are a threat to national security. No one knows you are here, and no one will know until after you are tried and hanged," Arthur replied.

"Give me your right hand," Jonas said.

"No. I will not submit to this procedure."

"It is painless. It only takes a second. I will make you if you do not comply," Jonas replied.

Jonas grabbed Liam by the arm, who tried to stand up. Arthur grabbed him and pushed him back into the chair.

Jonas splayed Liam's palm on the desk. He pushed down hard.

"Professor, please take the prints."

The professor was obviously used to criminals trying to avoid this new procedure. He was not worried by their protests.

The right hand was done quickly. The left hand was done easily. Liam had stopped wriggling.

"What use are they?" Liam asked. "They prove nothing." He seemed pleased with himself.

Arthur released Liam and said, "By themselves, the prints are irrelevant. However, when we compare them to prints on something you have touched, they become gold dust. We have three pistols from the flat where you were taken.

The numbers identified them from the Woolwich raid. Your prints will match those on the guns, and they will hang you. The professor assures me that no one has the same prints. Not even those we are related to. So, you see, it really is a waste of time denying the truth. The prints will convict you. We also know that you rented the flat in Covent Garden. We have witnesses. You cannot get away from the mounting evidence."

Liam said nothing as the professor and the two detectives left the cell. The professor went to the police laboratory in the basement and began to dust the weapons for prints.

Franz sat upright in the chair. He was not worried by the police. He had been questioned before, many times.

Jonas walked in first. "What is your name?"

Franz smiled. "I think you already know that."

"Yes, I know. But I would like you to confirm it."

"Detective?" Franz ventured.

"Detective Inspector Smethwick, of the City of London Police."

"Thank you, Inspector. I will not be answering any of your questions. You cannot make me."

"Believe me, Mr Mizel, I can, and I will."

"Inspector, I have been interrogated by some of the most obnoxious policemen in the world. I have been tortured by professionals. I did not break then and I will not now."

"We do not torture prisoners in England. But that does not mean I will not use other methods."

"Please look at my fingernails. There are none. They were pulled out by a German intelligence officer." He held his hands out for Jonas to see.

"My toenails are similarly gone. I have been burnt,

punched, near drowned and watched as my wife and child were killed in front of me. To my great shame, I did not break as they were murdered. What possible threat could you use against me?"

They sat opposite each other, eyes locked, staring. Each one unwilling to look away. The door opened and both men looked as a uniformed officer entered the room.

Arthur was ready to go through the same procedure as before. Jonas stood up and ushered him out of the cell.

"It is no good. He will not talk under any circumstances. Threats will not work. We need to come up with something he cares for."

"Family?" Arthur suggested.

"Murdered in front of him."

"All right, leave him to stew a little longer. Perhaps we will think of something. Time to see the sergeant major."

Brendan O'Carroll waited for someone to come in. Only one thing was on his mind: Mary-Jane. The door opened, both men entered. Brendan stood to attention.

"Sit down, Sergeant Major," Arthur said.

"Sir, you have to let me go. I know where Mary-Jane is. She is in danger. I beg you. I promise to return to custody after I have put her in a safe place."

"You are not going anywhere, O'Carroll. Except to a cell in the Tower, to await execution," Jonas said.

"Perhaps the sergeant major can help us a little more. No need to threaten."

"He cannot be trusted. Where has he been for the last three days? Hiding, that is where. No. Best let the gallows deal with him."

"Sergeant Major, are you willing to help us again?"

"Yes, but on one condition."

"You do not give us conditions. Constable, make arrangement for the prisoner to be taken to the Tower."

"At once, sir," the constable said, and went to leave the cell.

"Constable remain outside. Inspector remember your place. I am in charge of this prisoner."

"Sir, this prisoner has been arrested by me, for crimes committed under the jurisdiction of the City of London Police. I protest your interference."

"Outside, Inspector," Arthur said.

The constable re-entered the cell. "Well, what do you think?" Arthur asked.

"I think that O'Carroll will believe you are his friend. The question is, how do we exploit him?" Jonas said.

"I will go back. I will say that I have dismissed you. Then I can get any new information he has. We will take it from there. Agreed?"

"Agreed," said Jonas.

Arthur made a show of being annoyed as he entered the cell. "I am sorry about that. You did not have to see that. The inspector wants your head."

"That's all right, sir, I understand."

"Sergeant Major, I believe we can help each other. You want your wife back and I want to stop an attack against England. Will you help me?"

"Of course, sir. Save my Mary-Jane and I'll do anything you want."

"Good, good. Where is Mary-Jane being held? Tell me everything, the number of men, arms. Whatever you know."

Brendan told him the address, description of the building and what the old lady had said.

"Thank you, Sergeant Major, I will have Mary-Jane back by tomorrow. I promise. Now, tell me all that has happened since you went missing three days since."

Jonas and Arthur met in his room. "Did he go for it?"

"Yes. It seems that Mizel murdered one of his comrades for working for the Germans. I think we can use that as a lever."

"I cannot see him breaking over a murder allegation," Jonas replied.

"I was thinking that we could drive a wedge between the anarchist and Germans. It is obvious that Mizel does not like the Germans. The sergeant major said that the Germans had secretly financed the attack, but Mizel thought the money was coming from comrades in Europe."

"I see. So instead of a revolution, which would free the anarchists from oppression, they get a German takeover and end up imprisoned or shot. Both outcomes are chancy."

"Based on my knowledge of European anarchism, they hate the German state more than they hate capitalism."

"Maybe we can use that approach?"

Thirty-One
New Plan Formulated

Franz Mizel sat in another interrogation cell. This was better than he had visited. The walls were stone. The table and chair was attached to the floor by bolts. A single electric light bulb illuminated the whole drab room.

It was cold. He pulled his coat around him. His breath gave off a fine mist. He had been waiting hours. He knew this was an interrogation tactic. Cold, no food or drink. Silence. He had been through this many times. The silence was broken by the door being opened. The inspector he had spoken to before entered the room and sat opposite him.

"Grim room. My, it's cold. Would you like me to move you to somewhere more amenable? Just say the word. It can be done."

"I am fine. I am not bothered by this," Franz replied.

"I know that you will not break. Better men than me have failed. You will follow the sergeant major to the gallows. I can see from your expression you did not know. Yes, O'Carroll was hanged this morning for treason. It was not a pretty sight. You will be brought before a military tribunal this afternoon. It will be inevitable that you will hang tomorrow morning."

"I do not fear death. I have lived with it since I was a youngster in Poland. It matters not who does the deed; Russian, German, Polish or English. The only thing that matters is that you lived well. I do regret the demise of the sergeant major. He did not deserve to die like that. He was an innocent. He was caught up in a situation beyond his abilities. I truly believe he only wanted to save his wife. What will become of her, I wonder?"

"You are a rum character. You show empathy toward an individual, while plotting to kill thousands of innocents."

"In a revolution, there are casualties. You must expect that. I cannot expect you to understand."

"Oh, but I do. I am not ignorant of what happens in the world. I will do everything to stop your revolution. I will not shrink from killing all who come to my country to harm my people. But I believe you are a rank hypocrite. You speak of high-minded principles, yet you financed your attack from, probably the most reactionary country in the world: Germany."

"I was tricked. It is not my fault. You cannot blame me."

"Who else must I blame. You are the leader. You planned the attack, which will, if successful, allow the Kaiser to occupy England and its colonies. What will happen to your anarchist friends if that happens?"

Franz knew the truth of what Arthur was saying. The Germans would round up all of the anarchists and revolutionaries in England and perhaps Europe.

"There is nothing I can do. It is out of my hands. It is too late. The plans are too advanced to stop. I will not betray my comrades. I will die. No more questions."

"Yes, you will die, knowing that you have issued all your comrades with a death sentence. Think about that. I despise you. You are a coward."

Arthur left the room, leaving Franz to ponder what was said.

"Any luck?" Jonas asked.

"I am not sure. I think I got through, but I am worried. He seems to know that his revolution is doomed. He appears to accept it. He wants to die."

After two hours, a young constable approached Jonas and said, "Sir, the prisoner wishes to speak to you."

"Which one?" Jonas asked.

"The foreign gentleman, sir."

"Find Inspector Middleton. As soon as possible."

After speaking to Mizel all night, the plan was exposed. Mizel was candid. He gave names, addresses of all of the baron's men, hiding places and fellow travellers. He refused to name the anarchist involved.

***

Within the next week, raids were undertaken at the addresses given by Mizel. The results were disappointing. A few anarchists were arrested but they knew nothing of the planned attack. Some propaganda was taken. Underground flyers exhorted the faithful to be ready for the coming revolution. However, the police noted that the flyers were printed some years previously.

The press picked up on the raids. The general line was that the authorities were trying to ensure that troublemakers were controlled before the coming celebrations.

The streets around Tower Bridge were decked with union flags, bunting and new barriers. Army sentry posts were set up in strategic areas. Patriotic photographs of the royal family appeared in the windows of loyal subjects throughout London.

The bridge was adorned with huge flags and bunting. Workmen could be seen scrambling over the girders. Painters were touching up the crest on the bridge. Teams of sweepers were cleaning the roads leading to the bridge and Tower. Vendors from all over the country were arriving to find a suitable space to sell their wares to the crowds expected for the big day.

***

The police quietly rescued Mary-Jane. The two men holding her knew nothing of politics, they were local thugs hired to do a job.

Brendan and Mary-Jane were reunited the next day. They left for Clacton and her sister's home. After a week, Brendan was returned to London. His part of the bargain had to be paid.

Brendan was expected to re-join the conspirators. Jonas and Arthur were not sure that he would be allowed back in. Both thought that he would be killed as an informer. However, if he succeeded, they would, again, have an important line into the attack. If he failed, so be it. He was a murderer, after all.

Liam Cartney stood between two police officers in a dingy corridor. He was resigned to his fate. A door opened and the light streamed out. For a minute, Liam was blinded by the light. He heard a stern voice command, "Prisoner, quick march."

Liam recognised the man who entered the corridor. Brendan O'Carroll marched out, followed by two guards. Brendan waited as the guards cuffed his hands. They stood aside as Liam was marched into the room and the doors closed.

Liam stood in a courtroom. There was no jury. The tribunal members entered. An officer said, "All rise." The members took their seats. The tribunal were all high-ranking officers in the army.

The chairman, an officer from the General Staff, addressed the prisoner.

"Liam Cartney, you have been found guilty of treason. I sentence you to be hanged by the neck, until dead. Take the prisoner away."

Liam was unceremoniously marched out of the courtroom. He was shocked by its brevity. He knew that his life was over. The guards were uninterested in the proceedings. Liam asked the guard nearest him, "When?"

"Now. You're going to the Tower, where you will be executed immediately."

The guards led Liam to a waiting army lorry. He was helped into the back. He sat opposite Brendan. They looked at each other. They were left alone for a minute as the guards changed.

"I am to be hanged," the sergeant major said.

"I know, me too," Liam replied.

"I don't deserve this."

"None of us do," Liam said.

"I shall not die by the rope. I intend to run. A bullet in the back is preferable to the hangman's noose," the sergeant major said.

"And I shall help you." Liam smiled.

A guard shouted at the prisoners, "No talking."

Brendan began to twist the cuffs. His wrists began to bleed as he continued to try to open them. He had to stop when a guard climbed into the back of the lorry. He was armed with a rifle. He sat as far as possible from the prisoners.

The guard looked at the prisoners, then, satisfied that they would be no problem, relaxed. The lorry started to move forward.

"Corporal, how long to the prison?" Brendan asked.

"Half an hour. Now, no more questions." The guard seemed irritated.

"My rank is sergeant major. A bit of respect wouldn't come amiss."

"You were a sergeant major, you're my prisoner now. So be quiet. If I have to come over there, you'll regret it."

Brendan laughed, "Yeah, you and the Kaiser, no doubt."

The guard stood up, he held onto the swaying truck and moved towards the prisoners. He brought up the rifle butt to hit Brendan, who moved away from the guard. The corporal advanced. This was what Brendan had hoped for.

As the rifle butt was swung towards Brendan's head, he quickly moved aside. He grasped the butt and pulled it and the guard toward him. The man was not ready for Brendan's speedy tactics. With a twist of the butt, the rifle was pulled from his hands. Brendan quickly hit the man in the stomach. Liam jumped forward and pinned him to the ground, his hands over the prone guard's mouth.

Brendan placed his hands around the neck of the corporal and squeezed. Liam rummaged in his pockets for the keys to the cuffs. He quickly released his hands. Brendan let the guard fall. Liam unlocked Brendan's cuffs. Brendan cuffed the corporal and pushed a gag into his mouth. They both waited for the lorry to slow down. Liam moved the tail cover on the lorry. He noted that they were in the Strand.

He saw crowds of people, but no escort. Both men waited until the lorry slowed down at traffic lights and quickly jumped off the back, into the throng of people.

Thirty-Two
Betrayal

Superintendent Arthur Middleton and DI Jonas Smethwick sat together waiting for the call that would, they hoped, start the beginning of the end of the conspiracy. Up to now, they had plenty of information. Unfortunately, a large proportion was wrong, or had been changed by the conspirators.

The telephone rang, Arthur picked up the receiver, "Yes, I see. Is the guard hurt? Good, please put out an all-points bulletin. Descriptions of O'Carroll and Cartney to all forces. Please ensure that the ports to Ireland are checked. Thank you, Sergeant."

"It worked?" Jonas asked.

"Yes, O'Carroll and Cartney are free. I just hope the sergeant major does not double-cross us."

"Unlikely. We have Mary-Jane. It's more likely that he will be murdered by the baron's men, before he can contact us."

***

Liam and Brendan ran from the crowds and headed up Fleet Street. After ten minutes they slowed to a walk and used the back streets to get to Whitechapel Road. Off the main road, Liam stopped outside an old tenement block.

He told Brendan to wait while he went to an address in the block. After five minutes, he returned and told Brendan to follow him. They walked toward the Blackwall Tunnel. Directly opposite the entrance was another nondescript dwelling. Liam led the way.

Liam knocked quietly. The door opened and a man looked out.

Liam said, "Angel sent me."

The man said, "Who's he?" looking at Brendan.

"A friend of the cause."

The man scrutinised Brendan and finally decided to let both men enter.

Liam and Brendan walked in and were confronted by the man holding a pistol. He was quite short. The accent was East London. He had a roll-up cigarette hanging from the corner of his mouth. He was toothless and shabbily dressed. He coughed repeatedly, but never removed the cigarette.

"Sit down. Why are you here?"

"We escaped from the authorities. They were going to hang us. We need help to get out of London."

"This one looks like a Brit, ex-army, are you?" The man looked at Brendan. "You remind me of a bastard sergeant. Used to make my life hell. I hated him."

Brendan said nothing. The man spoke to Liam again. "I can help you. Not sure about him."

"He's already helped the cause. You can trust him. Check with Maitland or Graham. They know him," Liam replied.

"I will. You can stay the night. No going out or looking out of the windows. No noise. I've managed to stay free by never bringing attention to myself. And, by the way if I find out either of you are narks, I'll kill you."

Brendan found a corner of the flat and lay down. Liam took an old chair. The flat was sparsely furnished. It smelt of old liniment. The room was cold. The fire was out. A gas light spluttered as it gave out a faint light.

The man, whose name was Banham, retreated to his bedroom. He shut the door and pressed a chair against the handle. He sat on the bed looking at the door. The gun was nearby. After some time, he fell asleep.

The next morning Banham had gone. There was bread and jam on the kitchen table. They had something to eat and tried to decide what to do.

"Can he be trusted? I got the feeling that he would call the police if it suited him," Brendan remarked.

"I've known him for some time. I can't say he's a nice person. But he is committed to the cause. He lost his job in the docks years ago. He was agitator for the communist party."

Just then, the front door opened. The man walked in, followed by PC Maitland. He shook hands with Liam, then approached Brendan, "Sergeant Major, I thought you were dead."

For a moment, Brendan did not recognise PC Maitland. The short police hair cut had grown out. He now sported an impressive moustache. His hair had gone from a light brown to jet black.

"No, sir, we were arrested by the authorities and sentenced to death. We managed to get away."

"I see. That was lucky, wasn't it?" Maitland smiled.

Liam interjected, "Without the sergeant major, I would have been hanged, and you would have been led into a trap, organised by the baron."

For the rest of the morning, Liam told Maitland everything about Raul's part in the conspiracy. Brendan was able to fill in parts relating to the baron and his orders to spy on the anarchists and Friends of Hibernia.

Maitland was not surprised. "I have never really trusted the baron. The money he supplied was good, but he was never overgenerous. I thought something like this could happen. So, the baron intends to kill all my men and organise an invasion. Normally, the Brits getting a bloody nose would not bother me. But the massacre of decent Irish patriots cannot be allowed. The question is, what do we do now?"

"We have to abandon them. Let the Germans do what they want. We are not strong enough to take them on. You have seen their firepower," Liam said.

"No, all my lads are billeted with the Germans, awaiting the order to attack. If the baron got wind of our plans, he would eradicate them. I cannot take that chance. I need to speak to the FoH leadership and try to work out a plan to save our men, while appearing to support the baron."

Banham whispered to Maitland, who nodded. "We will have to move you to another safe house, Mr Banham is not comfortable with strangers."

***

Arthur and Jonas were seated in a secure office in the basement of Buckingham Palace. On a table were the plans of the king's itinerary for the celebrations at Tower Bridge. An army colonel was explaining the plans.

The equerry had been able to persuade His Majesty to accept a number of safe routes, should it become necessary. It was these that Jonas and Arthur were scrutinising.

The main route would be to lead the royal family away from the yacht, should it be attacked from the water. An armoured car would be stationed near St Olaf's dock. It would race to where HMY *Victoria and Albert* was berthed. A squad of guards would follow in a lorry. The retinue would then go to a secret destination.

"It looks safe. But what about an attack from the land?" Arthur asked.

"Members of the household cavalry will be stationed along the frontage of the wharves. Tooley Street will be closed off from Tower Bridge Road to Duke Street Hill. The London Bridge will have guards lined along the bridge, facing the Pool of London. Obviously, Tower Bridge will also be closed off at both ends. I can assure you; we have thought of everything," the colonel said.

"What of the proposed cruiser?" Jonas asked.

"Yes, I fear our naval friends may have been a little over

enthusiastic. We have had to downsize the patrols of the river. We looked at the tides and realised that the proposed cruiser would be unable to get into the Pool at low tide. We now have a smaller vessel, equally well armed, on its way from Portsmouth."

"Will the Pool be restricted?" Arthur enquired.

"Yes, we will have a barrage across the river. Only the yacht will be allowed in for the duration. The river police will ensure that nothing passes."

"What of the Tower of London?" Jonas enquired.

The colonel smiled. "That area will be shut to the public. Reinforcement will be billeted there. Motorised cavalry units will be ready to go to any area that needs help."

"Thank you, Colonel. It looks very professional. We will continue to track down the conspirators. Hopefully, the extra security will not be necessary." Arthur smiled and held his hand out.

"If you could keep me informed of your progress?"

"Of course," Arthur replied.

Both men left the palace and hailed a cab. Jonas said, "Well, what do you think?"

"I am not sure. On the surface it looks as if every conceivable contingency has been thought of. But I am still worried by the fire power of the barge. One or two shells fired into the Pool and all hell would break loose."

"I agree," said Jonas. "The trouble is, we do not know where the attack will start. If it is from water, the navy should be able to deal with the barge. But what if it is from the land? The king is vulnerable at several points; when he alights from the tender to Tower Bridge steps, and then to the bridge operations centre."

"I know. I have had many sleepless nights since finding out about the conspiracy."

"Of course, the one element that seems to have been ignored, is the public. There is likely to be thousands of men, women, and children, wishing to get near to the celebrations. It is likely that the roads will be blocked by the crowds. How can reinforcements get to deal with the attackers?"

"I spoke to the colonel about that very point. He seems to think that the crowds will be a hindrance to any attackers foolish enough to try and get away by land."

"How?" Jonas said, a little too loudly.

"I am not sure on that point. Perhaps he thinks that the crowds will stop the attackers."

"Does he know that the schools have been given a holiday to go to the festivities?"

Arthur said nothing. The two men looked out of the cab for the rest of the journey back to Scotland Yard.

Sitting in Arthur's office was DS Archie Routledge. Jonas walked in and saw him and rushed forward. "Archie, so good to see you. How are you?"

"Not too bad, sir. I've to take things easy for a few more months. The wound is healing nicely."

"DS Routledge, really good to see you." Arthur moved forward and shook Archie's hand.

"Thank you, sir. I was wondering how the case was progressing?"

"Not good, I am afraid," replied Arthur.

"We have been told not to tell anyone else."

"That's all right, sir. I understand. It's just that I can't help worrying."

"Now, Archie, your first priority is to get better. Leave the worrying to us," Jonas replied.

Arthur was smiling. He picked up a sheet of paper from his desk drawer. "I was waiting to tell you this. I had a note from the commissioner of police for the Met. In discussion with His Majesty, Detective Sergeant Archibald Routledge has been awarded the King's Commendation for Bravery. Congratulations Archie."

Arthur handed the paper to Archie. He took it and read it. He was speechless. Jonas and Arthur shook his hand.

"Obviously, the ceremony will take place after we have stopped this conspiracy."

***

Liam and O'Carroll were ensconced in a basement of a grand house in the home counties. Maitland had telephoned his superiors to alert them to the change of plan by the baron.

Maitland and Graham had been joined by the owner of the house, Sir Edward Byers, a notable pillar of the establishment and clandestine leader of the Friends of Hibernia in Great Britain.

They sat around a huge dining table. The blinds were drawn but the newly installed electric lights gave a welcoming glow to the room.

After a few minutes, the butler brought in more guests. In all, seven people now sat around the table. Sir Edward rose and began to speak.

"Gentlemen, our friends have brought worrying news of the machinations of our allies. Maitland, if you would?"

"Thank you, Sir Edward."

Maitland spent the next hour explaining and then answering questions concerning the new information. O'Carroll and Liam were brought before the men and questioned thoroughly by the group.

Brendan became the centre of attraction as he described the weapons available to the baron's men. As he had previously been briefed by Arthur and Jonas, he was able to draw the group's attention to the anarchists' involvement and subsequent in-fighting and murder of Raul Santiago.

Brendan was cleverly weaving a web of lies and half-truths to lure the FoH into breaking their commitment to the baron and the conspiracy. Liam was able to confirm the details that Brendan had said.

The main inquisitor was an American by the name of Cassidy. He was a leading fundraiser for the FoH in America. He was also a lawyer, quick witted and cynical about what he had heard.

"It seems to me that our plan is in danger of failing because of in-fighting. If we are believing the story we have been told, our lads' lives are on the line. And yet, I cannot believe that the baron would double-cross us. He needs our guys to make the plan work.

"I ask, what's in it for him? The Germans have no interest in Ireland. I have met the Kaiser, he assured me that Germany would remain a friend of the Irish people. No, we have to look deeper into the story. Who benefits if we attack the Germans? The Brits, that's who. Sounds very convenient, especially a week before the attack."

The group were silent, heads turned towards O'Carroll and Liam. It was Graham who broke the silence.

"I've seen the barge and can verify O'Carroll's description of the armaments. I do know that the number of Germans has multiplied since the barge was finished. They now outnumber us by at least three to one.

"This was not agreed by the leadership of the FoH. Our part was seen as an inspiration for all Irishmen around the world. If it succeeds, it will now be seen as a German victory. Our lads will be nothing more than cannon-fodder. Once again, Irishmen will be dying for someone else's cause."

Sir Edward asked the group what the next step should be.

Brendan had sat quietly throughout the discussion. He now asked to be heard.

"Sir, I know nothing of politics. My involvement in this affair was not planned. I am here through mistakes I made. And yet, I believe that the baron has tricked all of us. His dream, I believe, is the conquest of England. I know his opinion of those who are his allies. He has had me spying on Frank Mizel, and the FoH, for the last six months."

The group erupted into a mass of indignant cries. All eyes were on Brendan. Sir Edward was the first to call for calm.

"I suggest you need to explain yourself quickly or face the consequences."

Brendan knew that whatever he said needed to be believable, or he would not get out of the room alive.

"Sir, my wife, an innocent in this situation, was kidnapped by the baron's men. They made her watch as I was tied to a stake and shot in a mock execution. The implication was obvious, if I did not continue to spy on Franz Mizel, both I and Mary-Jane would be killed.

"Raul Santiago was a spy for the baron. Yes, he received money from the Germans to pay for the attack. But he also syphoned off money for his own use, which could have helped the FoH plan the attack more efficiently.

"Mizel had him followed. He denied knowing the baron despite being seen together. I was there when he was questioned. The anarchists and the FoH thought he was a Spanish man. In fact, he was a German. Mizel could not get his real name. Santiago refused to tell him anything, even after being tortured. Everything said was passed to the baron. He had a note from the Germans which was a death notice for the anarchists and FoH.

"I believe that the baron intends to massacre the volunteers and take credit for the overthrow of the government. With the success on the mainland, it would lead to an invasion of Northern Ireland, with all the benefits of its shipbuilding industry."

This last point had been a proposed by Arthur Middleton. It was hoped to sow the seed that Ireland would become part of an expanded German Empire.

"Thank you, Sergeant Major. Any questions?" Sir Edward said.

Cassidy started. "I do not know you, Sergeant Major, how come a newcomer seems to be able to worm into our business? What are your credentials? I need to know a lot more about you before I would want to believe you, son."

"Sir, I have already helped the FoH. I was at the Woolwich arms raid. I have killed two enemies of the Friends. PC Maitland can vouch for me. I tried to kill the baron after his men beat my wife and then kidnapped her. I have spied on the baron and told the FoH of his plans…"

Here, Cassidy interrupted, "And spied on us for the anarchists. Perhaps you have been spying on all of us for the Brits?"

"I have escaped from the rope with Liam Cartney. The first thing we did was to find PC Maitland and tell him of the baron's plans. We are here because we are loyal."

Cassidy stared at Brendan, unable to make his mind up. Brendan and Liam were told to go to the kitchen and await the council's decision. Liam and Brendan were brought back into the room where the FoH council were. Sir Edward addressed the throng,

"Gentlemen, after much discussion, we have decided that, despite the danger to our men, we have to remain in the plan. We will play our part. However, it now appears that our desires have become secondary to our German allies.

"This I will not countenance. Maitland and Graham will head a team of specialists. O'Carroll and Cartney will join this contingent; it will be responsible for the assassination of the royal family. The main attack will be led by the baron's men, as already planned. Maitland's team will infiltrate the wharf, opposite the yacht's berth.

"It is likely that the royal family will watch the bridge lift from the yacht. Seating has already been laid out for dignitaries. The cannon on the barge should take care of the king. For this to work, we must be ruthless. We cannot show any mercy. If we fail, we will all hang. Our men in Ireland will rebel as soon as news of the attack happens. Units in Dublin and Belfast will attack British barracks and prominent individuals. A proclamation will be read out in Dublin, declaring a free state. Good luck."

Thirty-Three
King For a Day

HMY *Albert and Victoria*, moved majestically upstream to the Pool of London. The king and queen were not aboard. The palace had finally agreed that the plot was to be taken seriously and took measures to discreetly protect the king.

The yacht was being shadowed by a contingent of police launches with armed officers aboard. It was past midnight when it approached Tower Bridge. The yacht would berth in the Pool of London. Access and egress from the yacht would be by tender. The date was June 28th.

Edward VII had never been more popular. His involvement in the entente cordiale had shown him to be a statesman of the highest order.

There were expected to be huge crowds in London. Licensed premises were given extended opening hours on the eve and day of the bridge celebrations. Fairs had arrived and set up on any free space.

The astute noticed the increased military activity in the streets surrounding London and Tower Bridges. This was expected. The military were cheered whenever they marched to their posts.

With the troops in place, a calm came over the whole area. Jonas and Arthur attended a last-minute briefing at the palace. The naval vessel heading for Tower Bridge had been delayed. It was hoped to get in position by ten am, when the king would enter the bridge's control room and press the button to raise the bridge.

***

In Buckingham Palace, the Honourable Giles Garlick was being helped to dress. Two of the king's courtiers were ensuring that he could pass muster as the monarch.

Giles had known the king since childhood. Giles' family were well respected members of the British aristocracy. Their lands and titles had been earned by choosing the winning side in the English civil war.

Giles had the misfortune to be born third in line to his family fortune. As with all of the gentry at that time, the eldest son inherited the title and wealth. Giles was ushered into the military.

His friendship with Edward VII was established after a shooting party at Sandringham. Giles was a seasoned drinker, smoker, and womaniser. The two men were the same age, liked the same sports and other activities and, from time to time, the same ladies.

Giles, it had to be said, looked like Edward. Although

taller, by two inches, he could easily pass as the king. In fact, they had swopped places on occasions; most notably at the changing of the guard ceremony, when the king was suffering from a hangover. Only the inner circle knew of these subterfuges.

Giles now stood in the full regalia of Edward VII. The courtiers stood back and examined every aspect of the vision in front of them.

The king and his equerry strode into the room. Edward looked at his friend. "Thank you, Giles, I will not forget this." He then shook hands with his friend and left the room.

The equerry smiled at Giles. "From now on, you are the king. No one outside these walls can ever know of this ruse. If you are wounded, you must function as his majesty would."

It was only now that Giles realised the importance of what he was to undertake. When it was suggested by the equerry that Giles stand in for His Majesty, he had not hesitated.

"I am curious, Sir Norbert, whose idea this was?"

"It was mine. His Majesty joked that perhaps we should get you to stand in. It was eminently a good idea, however, His Majesty was concerned that you could be harmed. The decision to go ahead would have to be your decision."

Luckily, he knew Edward, Bertie, to his friends, intimately. He was sure he could stand in for the king without anyone knowing.

Giles stood to attention as the national anthem was played. He was helped into the carriage that would take him to Tower Bridge. The horse guards surrounded the carriage and fell in to place as the phalanx left the confines of the palace.

Near Dagenham, a flotilla of eight Thames barges were lining up, two abreast. The sun was shining. A mist rose from the water. It would be a warm day. A slight breeze wafted across the barge's bow. Each captain had been vetted by the authorities and each barge had a pennant tied to the main mast, which showed it was an official part of the celebrations.

Two armed soldiers, dressed in full uniform, were stationed, one aft and one at the bow. All were heading for St Katherine Docks, where they would anchor on both sides of the river.

Following behind the flotilla was a Royal Navy frigate. Her crew were at action stations. The lookouts were stationed around the vessel, looking for the baron's barge. Others were watching ahead, trying to pinpoint firing points for the anarchists and Germans.

The wharves were adorned with flags and pennants hanging from every conceivable space. The roofs, cranes, and warehouse doors were locked down. No unauthorised persons were allowed to climb any structure. The crowds were already arriving and finding vantage points to see the pageant.

London Bridge had a line of troops next to the parapet overlooking the Pool. The crowds were pushing to see the yacht. Along the docks, crowds had infiltrated the waterfront and were climbing lamp posts and any available handhold to see the proceedings. As the police and soldiers removed them, more would take their place.

The police and army were trying to control the numbers

of people. However, the crowds were good natured, and a great deal of banter was exchanged between them.

Jonas Smethwick and Arthur Middleton were stationed at the city police incident room in the Tower of London, ironically by Traitor's Gate. They had news that the king was on his way.

***

As the king left for Tower Bridge, a contingent of twenty men, led by a sergeant major and accompanied by a police sergeant, approached a check point by St Olaf's Wharf. The sentry stepped forward and asked Brendan for his papers.

The papers showed orders for a punishment detail to clean the first floor of the building for an HQ. The orders were duly signed by a guards' colonel.

"Sorry, sir, I have to get this checked out by my officer, orders, sir."

"That's fine, Private. Perhaps you would like to join my men cleaning the latrines for the officers. I can always make room for one more," Brendan replied, menacingly.

The private was obviously worried, but a smile from Brendan made his mind up.

"Let them pass."

The men marched through the doors and up to the first floor. Brendan could be heard cursing them for their slovenliness.

Sergeant Maitland looked at the private. "Glad I'm only here to liaise. Seems to be a bit of a martinet."

"Yes, sir," the private replied, not wishing to be drawn.

The private made a note in his log, with the time and order number. He was relieved a little later.

Maitland quickly locked the doors behind him. They were heavy-duty iron gates to keep out thieves. The men began to barricade the doors and check out firing positions.

Brendan moved forward and looked out of a small window. He was looking down at the yacht. Soldiers were taking up their positions readying it for the VIPs. Guards were seen patrolling.

"Excuse me, Sergeant Graham, now we are here, where are the weapons?"

Graham walked up, dressed in fatigues, "Really, Sergeant Major, we are not a bunch of amateurs. They are behind that door over there." He pointed to another security cage in a corner.

They walked over as he took a keyring out of his pocket, opening the cage, he went to the iron gates and opened them. Inside was an arsenal of weapons. A quick glance showed machine guns, rifles, pistols, and grenades, of all types. The other men began to pull the weapons out, check them and load them.

Brendan was given a pistol. "I'm trusting you, Sergeant Major, don't let me down," Graham said.

"Sir!" Brendan replied. He walked over to a corner, sat down, and checked the pistol.

The others were quietly talking. They sat by their firing positions. No one smoked, although some wanted to. Maitland moved to the centre of the room.

"Have a nap, lads. No smoking or talking from now on. The patrols are due about now."

Brendan closed his eyes; He was thinking how he could get out of shooting anyone.

Maitland and Graham looked around the room at their men. They smiled. Liam was in a corner praying. When they saw Brendan, they took an extra-long look. He was their Achilles' heel. They had orders to kill him if he hesitated.

***

In a warehouse near the Erith Marshes, Udo Lebensberger mustered his men. They marched down to the barge. Each knew his job. Some removed the camouflage that had hidden the barge from the authorities and the curious. Others checked the munitions.

From a distance, the barge looked the same as the official barges. Close up, it was apparent that modifications had been made. The most important part of the plan was to disable the warship. Once this occurred, the barge would power to the bridge and open fire on the powerhouse. The king would not stand a chance.

When all the troops were aboard, Udo steered into the middle of the channel. He increased the speed to maximum.

In the warehouse, all was quiet. A patrol had checked the metal doors. Finding nothing, they moved on.

PC Maitland was looking down at the royal yacht. The viewing platform was slowly filling up. The yacht's tender drew alongside, and four military officers disembarked. The lesser members of the royal family were next to arrive.

A canopy was set in place over the seating. From where

Maitland was, the queen's seating was partially obscured. It did not matter; the bullets would rip through the canopy.

A line of soldiers in dress uniform lined up along the length of the yacht. They effectively formed a line of defence against anyone trying to board the yacht. On a given order, they turned and faced away from the royal family and guests.

Maitland and Graham were discussing the sight.

"Nothing to worry about. The first volley from the machine guns will deal with them."

Graham nodded to Maitland.

"Take your positions," Maitland said quietly.

The men went to their firing positions. Brendan stood in front of the doors, ready to repel anyone who managed to get through the barricade.

At ten o'clock, the king arrived at Tower Bridge. As he alighted the coach, a guards' band played the national anthem. Thousands of untrained voices joined in. An ear-splitting cheer rent the air when the anthem finished. After being introduced to various VIPs, the king was led onto the bridge. His entourage followed at a respectful distance.

At the entrance to the powerhouse, the king stopped and acknowledged the cheers of the crowds on both sides of the Thames.

The king visited the engine room and was shown the inner workings of the bridge. After a few questions about the mechanism of the bridge, he was taken to where he would press a button that would lift the bridge's arms.

In the warehouse, the men waited for the sound of the frigate being attacked. They knew that if the attack failed, the king would survive. Their job was to make sure the queen did not.

The king pressed the button. A bell in the engine room rang. The engineer released the steam, and the bridge arms began to rise. The crowds shouted in unison. There were smiles all round. The king was beaming, as was his entourage.

Thirty-Four
Death and Destruction

On the frigate, a lookout had spotted the baron's barge. The frigate's captain slowed down and was beginning to manoeuvre to face the barge.

Before he attacked, he wanted to be sure that it was hostile. It was a mistake. The cannon on the barge had a range of four thousand yards. Udo gave the order to fire.

A seven-pound shell hit the frigate just above the waterline, toward the stern. There was an immense explosion. Flames rose high. Udo followed up with another shell into the bridge. The vessel was effectively taken out of the conflagration.

The barge increased its speed. Its soldiers began firing the Maxim machine gun. Very quickly, the only sound from the vessel were the screams of the wounded and dying. Acrid black smoke rose from the frigate. All eyes were on the sinking ship.

Soldiers on both shores fired on the barge. Udo had expected this. He used the Maxim to clear a path on the south shore. He had the cannon loaded again and opened fire. This time the target was Tower Bridge.

Shouts and screams were heard as the crowds tried to find somewhere safe to hide.

The engine room was hit. The barge followed that up with a direct hit on the road span. The span was collapsing. The soldiers who had been stationed there were emptied into the Thames.

The screams of the dying, frightened people and the return of gun fire rent the air. Pandemonium had broken out. The crowds were fleeing the riverbanks and the bridges.

Unseen, the casualties from the first attack on the bridge were being helped away to ambulances. The king had felt the full force of the attack. He was mortally wounded. Even in the chaos, soldiers and civilians stopped what they were doing as the king was placed in an ambulance.

A shout was heard, "The king is dead." This echoed across the crowds.

In the German Embassy, a clerk was sending a coded message to the government in Berlin. Another coded message was sent to the Naval HQ in Bremen. The fleet was ordered to sea, destination England.

***

In the warehouse, the boom of the first shell was clearly heard.

"Open fire," shouted Graham.

On the yacht, the guests were all looking towards Tower Bridge. They could not see the frigate, but the noise of the explosion and billowing black smoke was clear.

The officer in charge on the yacht shouted for the queen and guests to leave the yacht and return to a safe house in the Tower of London. The soldiers who had lined the yacht's gunnels and formed a protective ring around the royal party.

As they started to move, the FoH volunteers opened up from the warehouse windows. Bodies were dropping all over the yacht. The protective ring was decimated within seconds. One volunteer shouted, "We got her. We got the queen." A spontaneous roar erupted.

"Quiet," Maitland ordered. "Continue firing. Leave no one alive."

Brendan tried to look out of a window, but the soldiers had reorganised and started firing at the warehouse. Volunteers began to fall. Maitland received a shot to the head; he spun around and was dead before he hit the floor.

"Sergeant Major, watch the doors." Graham pushed Brendan away from the window.

The doors were being attacked with hammers and pneumatic drills. The noise was overwhelming. Brendan glimpsed across at the volunteers, at least half were dead or dying. The others refused to give in.

The doors were beginning to bend and be forced in. Suddenly, the banging stopped. The force at the door had been withdrawn. Brendan thought they would use explosives to enter. He moved away and hid behind a concrete pillar.

"Sergeant Major, what's going on?"

"I think they're going to use explosives to get in," he replied.

Maitland blew a whistle. The volunteers stopped firing. "Get into the armoury. When the Brits come in, open fire."

***

As soon as the lieutenant in charge of the ceremonial guns heard the cannon, he ordered his men to load with high explosive shells. The blanks were quickly side-lined.

He heard and saw the royal yacht being fired on from the warehouse. A runner was dispatched to the officer in charge in the Tower. The orders came back, fire on the warehouse as soon as the troops attacking the first floor were pulled back.

Aware that the royal yacht was blocking the first floor, the lieutenant aimed two of his guns to bring the upper floors down onto the first floor.

The volunteers were ready for any eventuality, except that the army would try to bury them alive. At the same time London Bridge was hit the first time, two guns from the north bank opened fire. The upper floors took the full force of the cannons.

Inside the warehouse, they heard the blast and were covered with cement dust. The second blast was just seconds after the first. The upper floors collapsed on the volunteers. Those in the armoury were unable to move.

Brendan was thrown through a window onto Tooley Street. Graham was crushed under tonnes of brick and cement. The metal doors were crushed, and a gap appeared. A soldier crept in as far as possible. His flame thrower enveloped the free space in the warehouse. Those alive in the armoury were melted with the heat of the flames. The screams lasted a long time.

Brendan was arrested. Surprisingly, he was winded but not hurt substantially. He was bleeding from a head wound. From where he was sitting, he could hear the screaming of the volunteers burning.

"Is this the man?" an officer in a guard's uniform said. "Hold him for a summary courts martial." He walked away.

***

On the barge, Udo had steered past the frigate. He ordered the cannon to be loaded. The target was the troops on London Bridge. He could see that they were firing toward the warehouse.

The bridge was hit with two shells, which ripped a hole in the structure. As it hit, bodies flew into the air. The remaining troops retreated from the bridge.

He saw the ceremonial cannon shell the warehouse. He knew that the volunteers were dead. Using the collapsed road span as cover, he lined the barge up and gently turned it to point toward the ceremonial guns.

He knew that the British guns were far more powerful than anything he had, nevertheless, he was relying on a surprise shot. The German gunners, up to that time, had been exemplary.

"Men, you have earned the Kaiser's gratitude today. Two more targets and we will have done our job. Wipe out the cannons on the north bank. Then destroy the royal yacht.

The English will rue this day." Udo saluted them. They cheered him.

Police launches were heading for the barge, the officers were firing in unison. The Maxim opened up and cleared the last waterborne opposition.

Too late, the lieutenant saw the barge. The shell fell into the first two cannons. Metal and men were blown apart. A second shell decimated the remaining guns and men. The lieutenant was found by the Tower's wall.

On the royal yacht, the queen was being treated by the royal surgeon. Other casualties were being looked after by medics. They should have evacuated the yacht, but the onslaught from the warehouse and its collapse had blocked the escape route.

The first shell took out the bow. The second hit amidships. The yacht began to sink. People were trying to swim ashore. Ladies in formal gowns were sinking. The lounge where the queen was being treated had been set alight.

Volunteers from the guards were called upon to try to rescue the queen and entourage.

Brendan was sitting in the corner of a warehouse manager's room. Two soldiers were guarding him. "Can either of you men swim?" an officer enquired.

"Yes, sir," the corporal said.

"Right, get over to the royal yacht, Save as many as you can."

The officer looked at Brendan. "Name? Why are you wearing a uniform of the guard's regiment?"

Brendan tried to stand up but was pushed down by the remaining guard. "Sir, my name is Brendan O'Carroll, formerly sergeant major of the royal artillery. I am presently working for the Metropolitan police special branch, sir."

"This true, Private?"

"Sorry, sir, I really don't know. I was told to watch him. The other officer said to hold him for a courts, sir"

"It's true, sir, you can contact Detective Inspector Jonas Smethwick of the city police and Superintendent Middleton, of the special branch. I have news about the men behind this attack."

"What if I believe you? What are you doing here, now?"

"I had infiltrated the anarchists and German troops."

"You are telling me that the perpetrators are German?"

"It's true. The Germans, anarchists and the Friends of Hibernia are behind this attack. The German navy is sailing from Bremen, as we speak. They intend to invade England. The Kaiser would take over. I know it sounds mad, but it is true."

In the background could be heard gunfire and occasionally cannon fire.

"Private, watch him. I will be back as soon as I have verified this lunacy."

A quick call to the command centre saw Brendan, the officer and guard put in a cab. They drove to Dockhead, where they boarded a police launch. They were in the command centre within fifteen minutes. As they entered, Brendan was approached by DI Jonas Smethwick. "Nice to see you are still alive, Sergeant Major."

"Thank you, sir. The FoH contingent are dead. The warehouse collapsed on them."

"We know. How did you get out?"

"I was blown through a window. Very lucky, sir."

At that moment, Superintendent Arthur Middleton arrived with the king's equerry. "This way."

Arthur did not bother to acknowledge Brendan. They walked into a large room with various suits of armour on display.

The officer and guard were dismissed.

"Gentlemen, we need to be quick," the equerry said.

"Sergeant Major, you need to explain everything. Who is in charge on the barge? What did you mean about the German fleet? Everything, understand?"

"The captain of the barge is called Udo Lebensberger. He is a German naval officer. He has orders to kill the king and queen. I saw his orders from the baron while I was working on the barge. He's not concerned if he lives or dies."

"You helped to outfit the barge?" The equerry was incredulous.

"Sir," said Arthur, "we can discuss that later. We need to know about what else we can expect."

Brendan continued. "Udo will continue to attack everyone and everything until he runs out of ammunition. You have to blow him out of the water."

"Easier said than done. He destroyed the frigate and the royal yacht. Our ceremonial cannons have been obliterated. Our artillery pieces are too powerful to use across the Thames. We could take out hundreds of people."

The equerry seemed unable to understand the situation.

"Sir, if I may? The cannon on the barge, the Tower armoury has one. It is powerful enough to hole the barge, without passing through the hull. A shot midships would hit the ammunition. It would explode into a thousand pieces."

In the background, they could hear as another shell was fired into Tower Bridge. Immediately afterwards the Tower itself was hit. Udo was determined to wipe out everything he could.

Despite being hit with machine-gun fire, the barge was remarkably strong. The iron gunwale was doing its job. Udo had lost some men, but every time the army had tried to fire down on them, Udo had replied with the Maxim or the cannon.

"We have no choice. Sergeant Major, go with these men. Collect the cannon and destroy this menace." The equerry demanded.

The machine gunners on the barge were busily keeping the troops' heads down. It was frustrating the barge was still whole and capable. Snipers in the Tower were having some success, until Udo returned fire from the cannon.

Brendan had found the cannon with help from the keeper of the armoury. Twenty men manhandled it across to St Katherine Docks. Brendan only had nine shells to use: part of the display. He had no idea if they would explode.

Udo kept the barge moving. His ammunition was quickly being used. The shells lay across the bottom of the hull in neat rows. He had no idea that danger was coming from behind.

Brendan had the wheels chocked and lined the cannon up. He was aiming for the middle of the barge. He stepped back and pulled the lanyard.

The shell exploded from the barrel. It hit the barge on the aft. The Maxim was wiped out, its crew killed. Udo was knocked off his feet. He lay on top of his supply of shells. His face was covered in blood. He ran toward the hold, he pulled a cable, it began to fizzle. The cord slowly burnt its way to the dynamite stored along the keel.

Udo shouted to abandon ship. He crawled to the aft and jumped into the water. He swam toward the south bank.

The barge's steering had been removed. Water was pouring in through the gash in its side. The cannon was pointing away from the attackers.

Brendan realigned the cannon, reloaded, and made sure it was pointing in the right place. Once again, the shell was fired into the barge. There was a massive explosion as the barge blew into pieces. It was not known whether it was the shell or the dynamite igniting, the result was the same.

When the dust and smoke had settled down, everything was smashed. Bits of bodies fell to earth and joined the flotsam in the river. A cheer went up from all the troops on either side of the river. It was quiet soon after, as the army counted the cost of the attack.

The bells of St Paul's began to ring. Other bells from churches all over London rang out spontaneously. The joy turned to sadness as the people realised that the king and queen had been killed. Sadness turned to fury as foreigners were attacked. It did not matter if they were Germans or not. Someone had to pay.

***

In the North Sea, the German fleet were met with a line astern of ships of the Royal Navy. The standoff did not last long. The German fleet returned to base.

In Buckingham Palace, Edward VII was saddened by

the news of the deaths of Giles Garlick and Lady Florence Beaumont, the latter standing in for Queen Alexandra.

However, he needed to reassure the nation that he was still alive. But first, he called the Kaiser. Only the closest aides knew what was said, but Edward was clear that future relations would be harmed if it were shown that he, the Kaiser, had known of the attack. Assurances were given.

The press of the empire and world were invited to Buckingham Palace to meet the sovereign, to assure them of the Royal family's continued safety.

Every embassy in the world had a prearranged statement issued concerning the events of June 30th, 1904.

Almost at once, after the attack had ended by Brendan's actions, the civilian authorities took over the hunt for the other conspirators.

Brendan was taken back to Scotland Yard. He was put in an interrogation room, to await his fate. DI Smethwick entered the room, Brendan stood up.

"Sergeant Major, we have a number of questions for you. Please sit down. Why didn't you contact us before the attack?"

"I was unable to, sir. Graham and Maitland effectively kept me locked up. When we arrived at the warehouse, we were locked in. They did not trust me, sir."

"What happened to them?"

"Graham and Maitland died when the roof collapsed. The priest also died. He was hit by a bullet from the army."

"Good, so Liam Cartney too. What about Baron von Marburg?"

"I believe he returned to Germany. I'm not sure, sir. There are more conspirators, sir."

"What do you mean?"

"The leaders of the Friends of Hibernia, sir. I met them in a country house, just outside London. The leader of the FoH is Sir Edward Byers."

"Are you sure?"

"Yes, sir."

"Write down anything else you can remember. I will be back."

Jonas contacted Arthur Middleton. He told him of Sir Edward's involvement. A detachment of armed officers was sent to arrest Sir Edward. Ports to Ireland and the continent were closed.

In Tring, Sir Edward was awaiting news of the attack. A news blackout had been imposed as soon as the attack had started. Sir Edward had his carriage loaded with essentials. His plan, if the attack failed, was to travel to the east coast where a vessel would take him to the continent. He would then travel to a new life in America.

If the attack succeeded, he would meet Baron von Marburg at Harwich. He would then join the Kaiser's army and be part of the new German administration.

The other members of the FoH council had already left for Liverpool. Arrangements had been made to organise the volunteers in Ireland.

***

In Ireland, the administration had been warned about the attack. At midnight, Dublin and Belfast had been swamped with British Army units. The ports had been locked down. Snatch squads had started to arrest volunteers and sympathisers.

In the countryside, volunteer units had met British Army units ready for anything. The revolution was stopped before it had a chance to start. Throughout the empire, troops had also been put on alert.

Arthur Middleton was leading several units of the army and police officers, to arrest Sir Edward Byers. In the quiet countryside of Tring, news was trickling into the area. No one could verify that the king and queen had been killed. Locals came out to gossip. The local police had been given orders not to allow crowds to amass.

Four lorryloads of heavily armed personnel drove through the village, heading for Sir Edward's estate. The locals returned to their homes.

Sir Edward's carriage was driven slowly out of the estate's huge gates. As several police officers surrounded it, it became clear that Sir Edward was not in it. The troops and Middleton surrounded the manor. Middleton entered the manor and called for Sir Edward.

A shot was heard from the study. Sir Edward had seen the troops and police arrive. He was determined not to face the ignominy of a trial and execution.

Middleton swore. "All right, check the manor. Lieutenant, secure the building. My officers, search for any documentation."

In the cellar, servants were burning documents. They were arrested and taken away. The gamekeeper had started a fire in the servants' kitchen. Within minutes the manor was engulfed in roaring flames. Everyone managed to get out.

The gamekeeper, however, chose to fight. He was shot down by the army.

Middleton gathered his men and headed to the local police station where the servants were handed over to the sergeant. They were released after it was proved they had no part in the conspiracy.

***

In London, the news of the royal family's escape was telegraphed around the world. In Fleet Street, photographs of the king and queen were handed out to the public. Over the next week, the main headline in all of the newspapers was about the royal family. Normality was the desired aim.

In various jails around the country, conspirators were being questioned. The higher echelons, leaders of the FoH, were tried by courts martial. They were shot at dawn by firing squad.

Franz Mizel had been told of the failure of the coup. He was not surprised. He asked to see Superintendent Middleton.

DI Jonas Smethwick went with Arthur Middleton to Paddington Green, where Franz was being held.

"I hope you are not going to plead for your life?" Arthur said.

"No, I believe my time has come. However, I wish to leave this existence with a clear conscience."

"How very noble of you," Jonas muttered.

"I make no excuses for my actions. We are at war with the reactionary forces of the world…"

"Oh, please, save the speeches," Arthur interrupted.

"Force of habit. I know where the baron is. I only ask that I be shot, rather than hanged, in return."

"What makes you think we would deal with you?"

"I think you would want the baron more than me."

"I cannot promise anything, but I will try."

"Good, he is holed up in a cottage near Norwich. I can show you on a map. He has an entourage of three armed men."

Thirty-Five

Mopping Up Begins

U do swam to the nearest ladder fixed to the wharf's wall. He wearily hauled himself up the rungs. As he reached the top, he rolled over to the safety of the parapet. He lay there for a few minutes, trying to get his breath back.

The wharf was quiet. Udo removed his jumper and turned it inside out. The gold ring on his cuff showed the rank of lieutenant. He hoped that no one would question his rank. It was solely to get through any cordon.

As he stood up, he viewed the carnage he had committed. The frigate was on its side, black smoke still spewing out. The barge had sunk, only pieces were left floating amid the bodies of those who had failed to get off quickly enough. The royal yacht was listing heavily. Fire and smoke was being tackled by the fire brigade. Screams were still heard as victims were treated.

He turned and walked away. As he approached a gate,

a police officer was staring at him. "Officer, could you open the gate, please? I am a survivor from HMS *Braveheart*."

The officer moved forward to the gate, "Do you have any ID, sir?"

"Afraid not, I Just managed to get off the ship before it sunk. I am soaking wet, cold, and ashamed we did not stop the attack."

The officer took a key off of a ring and opened the gate.

"There's no reason to be ashamed, sir. Your ship fought well, in the traditions of the Royal Navy. Do you need a blanket?"

"Thank you, Officer, most kind. I need to get back to my ship's company, or what is left of it. Is there any transport available?"

A small crowd had gathered and were listening to the conversation. A man stepped forward, "I would be honoured to help you, sir. I've a taxi across the road. I'll take you."

"Thank you. I need to get over the river to Wapping, I believe my company is waiting there."

"No problem, I'll get you there. Is that okay, Officer?"

The police officer looked at Udo, he certainly looked the part. His accent was spot on for a naval officer. He had no reason to doubt him.

The police officer agreed. Udo shook his hand and walked over to the taxi. Within minutes, Udo and the driver were heading away from the scene of the action.

Baron von Marburg was waiting impatiently for news of the attack. A telegram arrived at his hotel. The baron read the one word. 'eins'. This meant that the king was dead.

Soon after, another telegram arrived, 'Admiral'. The fleet

was on its way to England. The baron stood up and walked to the window overlooking the North Sea. He smiled.

There was a knock at the door, his aide opened it. A third telegram had arrived. It simply read 'eins+eins'. He knew that the queen had also died. Feeling that the operation had succeeded he dressed in the full regalia of a colonel in the cavalry to await the German troops being transported to the coast.

The authorities in London had telegraphed information to the whole country. Telegraph wires were singing with the news that the coup had failed. Every newspaper, local or national, showed photographs of the royal family standing outside Buckingham Palace. Reporters were verifying that the king and queen were safe. They hinted that an extraordinary piece of news would be forthcoming soon.

The baron received a copy of the local paper, the *Harwich Sentinel*. The headline read: 'Royal Family, safe and well'. He read the front page, starting a paragraph and then moved to another. He screwed the paper into a ball and threw it across the room.

He called his aide, "Get the carriage ready. We are moving."

The baron quickly changed again. He dressed in a fairly staid, dark suit. Within ten minutes he was ensconced in a carriage heading for Felixstowe. A German fishing boat was just off the coast, ready to pick him up. He hoped that travelling by carriage would throw off the authorities. They would expect him to use a faster mode of transport.

Two hours after the baron had left, a detachment of soldiers and police had arrived at the hotel. Descriptions were taken, and orders were passed to a squad of soldiers led by a lieutenant from a shadowy unit. They drove off in an unmarked army lorry, in hot pursuit.

London returned to its business fairly quickly. Contracts were awarded, Tower and London Bridges were cleared of debris and renovation started.

In a cell in Scotland Yard, Brendan O'Carroll sat holding hands with Mary-Jane. He was awaiting his fate. He had caused the authorities a good deal of soul-searching. The king wanted to award him with a gallantry medal. The press had managed to get a photograph of him aiming the cannon at the barge. He was being lauded as a hero.

Someone had been leaking information about his exploits as a spy against the anarchist and Irish rebels. The German involvement had quietly been forgotten. It was thought that some remnants of the Friends of Hibernia were still protecting Brendan.

DI Jonas Smethwick was livid. He had an iron-clad statement from O'Carroll that he had murdered three people. But his superiors were reluctant to send him to trial. The pressure was growing on him to take a step back.

Superintendent Arthur Middleton was also feeling pressure from his bosses. The two men met up at the pie house.

"I wish I had not used O'Carroll in this whole affair. I should have had him tried and hanged," Jonas said.

"I know. It seems that the security service is looking at him. They think he could be useful to them."

"My God, he murdered three men, two of whom were police officers. I cannot stand by while he is lauded as a hero."

"Unfortunately, it looks like he will get away with the Puddle Dock murders. He is more useful as a hero than a murderer. My boss let it slip that the palace and government are extremely worried that he could mention the German involvement."

"What about a closed trial? Over very soon and then shot. Tell the world he died of injuries received. Still a hero but a quiet one," Jonas suggested.

"I received a missive from my director, after reading my interim report he ventures an opinion which will not please you."

"Can you tell me?" Jonas asked.

"He noted that without the Hetherington murder, the authorities would not have found out about the conspiracy. The Friends of Hibernia would not have taken an interest in O'Carroll. Therefore, he would not have come into contact with the baron or the anarchists. It is likely that the king would have been assassinated. The Germans would have invaded, and England would now be a principality of the German Empire."

"My God, are you serious?"

"If you view it logically it does make sense. My director has recommended no action against O'Carroll. That view may be tempered by his desire to use him in the future."

"Is there nothing we can do?"

"I am afraid it is outside our hands. I hear the royal family will attend a service at Westminster Abbey, to give thanks that the king and queen survived."

"I can understand that, but please, O'Carroll will not be there?"

"Somewhere near the back, sorry." Arthur laughed. "Changing the subject slightly, Franz Mizel was executed by firing squad this morning. I am told he made an impassioned plea for the revolution, before being told to be quiet."

"Any news on the baron?" Jonas asked.

"No, It seems he managed to get to a fishing boat near Lowestoft. We suspect he is in Germany. Oh, guess who was picked up last week?"

Jonas was in the mood for quizzes. "No idea, who?"

"Udo Lebensberger, the baron's man. The leader of the attack and captain of the barge. He was caught driving a taxi toward Harwich. It seems he robbed and killed the driver. He will be passed over to the German authorities for punishment. He will be shot as soon as he has been interrogated. They have promised."

"I wish we had the baron," Jonas replied.

"By the by, I have been promoted to chief superintendent."

"Congratulations, Arthur. Well deserved."

"Any news for yourself?"

"Nothing, I think I may have upset the brass for my demand to have O'Carroll tried."

"Move on. We are mopping up the small fish. My office has been inundated with all sorts of requests to join the service. We could use a talented officer with detection experience?"

"Are you offering me a job?"

"Yes, I have cleared it with my boss. How does Superintendent Jonas Smethwick sound? You would also need a good sergeant."

"You mean I could have Archie?"

"Absolutely, I took the liberty of already asking him. He has agreed if you give permission."

Over the following weeks, the press were briefed about the sacrifice of Giles Garlick and Lady Florence Beaumont. They were hailed as heroes by the press.

Approximately three months later, Brendon O'Carroll stood before the king. He was decked out in his uniform, pressed to perfection by Mary-Jane.

He received the King's Medal for Gallantry. Archie received his medal next. After the ceremony, Brendan and Mary-Jane were whisked away by two officers of the security service.

As soon as Jonas had moved to the special branch, he received his own gallantry medal.

In Paderborn, Germany, a dishevelled old gentleman smoked a last cigar, it was Cuban. The arrogance of his former authority still showed through. He was dressed in workingman's overalls. He nodded his head towards the major in charge of the firing squad.

Baron von Marburg dropped his cigar and squashed it under his heel. Two men moved forward and tied his hand to the stake. He refused a blindfold. Twelve rifles fired simultaneously. The baron gasped as they hit their target. He was dead before the major needed to administer the coup de grâs.

As per the Kaiser's instructions, the baron was buried in an unmarked grave. Udo Lebensberger died under interrogation. No one knows where he was buried.

One year after the attack in London, the two bridges were officially reopened. The king's special guest was Kaiser Wilhelm II, Emperor of Greater Germany. The crowds greeted him as an honoured friend.

Brendan and Mary-Jane were moving to India. They were driven to Southampton. They boarded the *India Star* and taken to their second-class cabin. The cabin boy stood aside as Brendan inspected their temporary home.

Brendan gave the young lad a penny. Mary-Jane sat on a plush armchair. She absent-mindedly stroked the red material. Brendan smiled. They were going to India where Brendan was to keep an eye on disaffected soldiers and tribesmen.

He sat on the settee. He patted the seat next to him. Mary-Jane moved and sat next to him. He held her hand.

"Now, dearest, what news?" They both smiled. She handed him a newspaper. He began to read the headlines.

The ship's klaxon was heard as the ship slowly eased away from the dock.